The New Puritan Manifesto

1. Primarily story-tellers, we are dedicated to the narrative form.

2. We are prose writers and recognise that prose is the dominant form of expression. For this reason we shun poetry and poetic licence in all its forms.

3. While acknowledging the value of genre fiction, whether classical or modern, we will always move towards new openings, rupturing existing genre expectations.

4. We believe in textual simplicity and vow to avoid all devices of voice: rhetoric, authorial asides.

5. In the name of clarity, we recognise the importance of temporal linearity and eschew flashbacks, dual temporal narratives and foreshadowing.

6. We believe in grammatical purity and avoid any elaborate punctuation.

7. We recognise that published works are also historical documents. As fragments of our time, all our texts are dated and set in the present day. All products, places, artists and objects named are real.

8. As faithful representations of the present, our texts will avoid all improbable or unknowable speculation about the past or the future.

9. We are moralists, so all texts feature a recognisable ethical reality.

10. Nevertheless, our aim is integrity of expression, above and beyond any commitment to form.

All Hail the New Puritans

EDITED BY NICHOLAS BLINCOE AND MATT THORNE

FOURTH ESTATE • *London*

This paperback edition first published in 2001
First published in Great Britain in 2000 by
Fourth Estate
A Division of HarperCollins*Publishers*
77–85 Fulham Palace Road
London W6 8JB
www.4thestate.co.uk

Contents

Introduction: The Pledge

NICHOLAS BLINCOE AND MATT THORNE

Fifteen writers; ten rules. The aim of this anthology was to bring together a group of like-minded writers and set them a challenge. Strip their fiction down to the basics, and see if something exciting emerges. The idea was partly playful, but equally serious. The rules were designed to emphasise what makes recent fiction so original and challenging. They had the unintended benefit of making it impossible for a writer to submit a story from their bottom drawer. Every story here was written for the anthology and, taken together, this collection shows how British fiction is currently among the most exciting in the world.

The title *All Hail the New Puritans* is taken from a song by The Fall. This is not a religious movement. It could, however, be the beginning of a new wave. A chance to blow the dinosaurs out of the water.

These are the rules, and our thinking behind them:

1 PRIMARILY STORY-TELLERS, WE ARE DEDICATED TO THE NARRATIVE FORM.

Nicholas: Fiction becomes seductive at the moment a story begins to unfold. This seems so obvious, I wonder how it ever came to be a contentious point. What is it that makes fiction compelling, if not the story-line? Of course, we can talk about the beauty of individual phrases, even the pleasure of the text. But the pleasure comes through the story-telling. Narrative is the life force of fiction, and without narrative the most attractive constellations of words or the most carefully poised sentences are nothing but make-up on a corpse.

Matt: Whenever people have tried to defend story-telling in the past, they have turned to supposed 'traditions'. Parables and folk-tales; fables, jokes and moral instruction. But we aren't using history as a justification. Story-telling does not need the validation of tradition. New Puritanism is about looking to the future.

Nicholas: Reading these stories, I was reminded, over and over, of what I love in fiction. The language of great fiction may be beautiful or barbaric, it might be witless or erudite, whatever it takes to tell the story. Of course the quality of the language matters, but only in a strictly limited sense, because it is always subordinate to the overall form, the big picture. While I admire the formal experiments of writers like B. S. Johnson, Italo Calvino or Georges Perec, the stories in this collection prove that the most subtle and innovative form available to the prose writers is always going to be a plot-line.

2 WE ARE PROSE WRITERS AND RECOGNISE THAT PROSE IS THE DOMINANT FORM OF EXPRESSION. FOR THIS REASON WE SHUN POETRY AND POETIC LICENCE IN ALL ITS FORMS.

Matt: Looking through these stories, it quickly becomes clear that poetry is less of an influence than film, technology, music or television. Fiction must always try to define the prominent cultural forms of its time. Today, fiction should be focusing on the dominance of visual culture, and attempting to prove itself the equal of these mediums.

Nicholas: Film undeniably enjoys a kind of cultural primacy – at least it did in the twentieth century. Without doubt, this represents a positive challenge, reminding writers that fiction must constantly reinvent itself, as other technologies deliver new ways to tell stories.

Yet no matter how much I love films, I believe that prose fiction remains the inspiration for all other kinds of story-telling. Throughout the evolution of cinema, from the near-clockwork technology of film projection, through analogue television to digital images, the goal has always been a friction-free, infinitely flexible way to deliver stories. And the fiction writer has always had access to this technology: the purely conceptual, even virtual, motor of the story-line.

Matt: Fiction is the most immediate form of expression. Anyone who has tried to get a film through to production has probably faced all kinds of compromises that (most of the time) can be avoided in fiction.

Nicholas: This rule is also the one that distinguishes between fiction and poetry. There is a traditional hierarchy that places poetry above prose. Poetry is divine because it is beautiful, rising above the mundane as it aspires to pure meaning. In contrast, prose is prosaic, worldly, flattened by its obsession with the everyday. One response to this hierarchy is to argue that fiction can compare with poetry. Previous generations of writers have actively sought an association with poetry movements. The puritan response is different: it completely rejects the classical hierarchy. Poetry is so different to prose, it has nothing to offer or to teach the prose writer.

Matt: I have never been able to look at modern poetry without thinking of it in an academic way. The retreat to the campus has meant that poetry has lost its primacy as a cultural form. It is not the way we think, and it is not the way we write. It is impossible to write verse without turning life into artifice. Maybe the same is true of prose, but great fiction recreates the immediacy and the rhythm of life itself instead of small, frozen movements.

3 **WHILE ACKNOWLEDGING THE VALUE OF GENRE FICTION, WHETHER CLASSICAL OR MODERN, WE WILL ALWAYS MOVE TOWARDS NEW OPENINGS, RUPTURING EXISTING GENRE EXPECTATIONS.**

Nicholas: Genres are useful, but only at the level of taxonomy. I would be as lost in a library that ignored genres as I would be in a record store that mixed the soul section with the metal. Similarities exist between different books but, once I have made a selection, I am not looking for similitude. I am looking for a difference. Anyone who loves fiction, loves the things that they have never read before.

It has often been argued that there are a finite number of plots. The exact numbers often change ... that there are only seven adventure stories, or only three love stories, or only one crime story. No one who cares for fiction could seriously advance this kind of argument. Narrative is essentially flexible, it is flexible at its very core. In the end, stories resist any attempt to categorise them. Think, again, of poetry. A sonnet will always be similar to another sonnet: there are rules and they have to be obeyed. In aspiring to eternal ideals, poetry requires forms that are rigid and unyielding. Poetry is defined by metre – ultimately by the stomp of jackboots. But fiction is defined through rhythm, the syncopated pacing of a plot. Fiction is both profligate and perverse, always spinning off into new directions.

Matt: I think we've moved through the excitement of seeing old genres subverted, reinvented and modernised. The challenge now is working out what from this intellectual exercise remains useful to us. We can still write from experience; it is just that our experience has been enriched by modern culture's constantly changing hall of mirrors. The films we've seen, the books we've read, the games we've played: these are all now a part of our available autobiography. And, most of the time, there's no reason to play it straight.

Nicholas: A story-line is always an escape plot. Too often, any tendency towards escapism in fiction is treated with suspicion. At its worst, this suspicion is extended to literature as a whole, so that it embodies a desire to retreat from reality into a dream world of romance or adventure. I think this is the result of a misunderstanding. The truth is not that fiction can be escapist, but that fiction embodies a desire for freedom.

4 **WE BELIEVE IN TEXTUAL SIMPLICITY AND VOW TO AVOID ALL DEVICES OF VOICE: RHETORIC, AUTHORIAL ASIDES.**

Matt: The challenge presented by this rule is to get everything into the story. There can be nothing in inverted commas, and the reader gets to choose how to read each line. Too many writers get caught up in the cult of the personality, to the point where readers remember the names of authors but not the books they are supposedly famous for. And authorial asides are just a classy way of digging someone in the ribs.

Nicholas: What happens to authors when they want to express their opinions? They might write lengthy, bullet-pointed introductions. Or they could become like Norman Mailer ... I doubt there is a writer alive who cannot sympathise with the impulse to use their novels as a platform for rants and tirades. But a puritan aims to write pure fiction. And fiction is never about grandstanding in the debating chambers, trying to speak for a generation or win over public opinion.

Today, biography and political essays seem to be the highest form of literature. They receive the most prominent reviews, the writers receive the highest honours. As though the role of literature is to honour legislators and orators and respect the institutions and establishments that support them. Real literature, drama and fiction, are incapable of celebrating any establishment. Because stories are about change and escape, fiction can only speak about the processes that modify or erode institutions; even, at times, destroy them.

5 **IN THE NAME OF CLARITY, WE RECOGNISE THE IMPORTANCE OF TEMPORAL LINEARITY AND ESCHEW FLASHBACKS, DUAL TEMPORAL NARRATIVES AND FORESHADOWING.**

Nicholas: There are many examples of great literature that use dual narratives, flashbacks, and other effects that aim at unsettling notions of identity and of time. So the fifth rule could be seen as perverse. And yet ...

Flashback is a device that aims to imitate memory. Yet

memory remains a much misunderstood phenomenon. In fiction, as in life, we are tempted to regard memory as a reservoir of images. The pool is there, ready and waiting, and all we need to do is throw in a bucket and dredge up the appropriate recollection. The truth is very different. Memory is an activity and memories cannot exist independently from the process of remembering. In effect, the act of remembrance creates memories, whether this act is conscious or unconscious. This is why the flashback is so problematic – it never occurs as part of an action, it is simply parachuted in from above. Flashbacks are essentially undramatic because they do not imply any activity. This rule puts the focus back on the drama behind every action.

Matt: Flashbacks are a cheap trick. And the risk of a temporal shift rarely pays off. Giving the reader information from events before the story started is an artificial way of deepening a character's psychology: if the characters are strong, we need only know what they're doing now. Leave the psychoanalysis to the literary critics.

Nicholas: In any sequence of events, the last events will always, in some way, be related to the earlier ones. Even if they are not triggered by the earlier events, the very fact that they form a sequence implies a relation, at least of proximity. But there is a value in attempting to avoid foreshadowing, at least because foreshadowing goes hand-in-hand with dramatic irony. It cannot be said too strongly: the very concept of dramatic irony is an oxymoron. Irony defuses any sense of drama because it announces what to expect before it happens. From the outset, *Time's Arrow* told us that the Holocaust is very like a process of creation, except in reverse. Just as *Midnight's Children* told us that a nose can be very like the sub-continent of India, foreshadowing partition in its very membrane. But once these declarations have been made, where is the insight, where the revelation? Avoiding foreshadowing means puffing the sense of surprise back into fiction.

Matt: I have no problem with dual narratives generally, especially in longer fiction. But for this project we wanted to force the included writers into putting everything into a single narrative strand. The intention behind this was to encourage a simplicity and solidity that would ensure each story remained enjoyably direct.

6   WE BELIEVE IN GRAMMATICAL PURITY AND AVOID ANY ELABORATE PUNCTUATION.

Matt: Obscurantism has long since fallen out of fashion. The only elaborate punctuation that still seems to attract a large number of contemporary writers is parentheses, perhaps because we live in an age which encourages querulousness. Grammar and syntax go hand in hand to create the simple or complex world of the novel − the building blocks of story-telling should not be focusing on the minutiae of narrative but the grand plan.

7   WE RECOGNISE THAT PUBLISHED WORKS ARE ALSO HISTORICAL DOCUMENTS. AS FRAGMENTS OF TIME, ALL OUR TEXTS ARE DATED AND SET IN THE PRESENT DAY. ALL PRODUCTS, PLACES, ARTISTS AND OBJECTS NAMED ARE REAL.

Nicholas: There are two crucially important reasons why fiction needs to return to a real sense of the contemporary; even to name-checking products and places and names. First, there is the question of judgement. The final judge of a writer is the reader, and together the writer and the reader share a world. There is a marked tendency of authors to set contemporary fiction in a parallel reality: one where car names are slightly modified, the pop stars are slightly different, the slang is artificially modified. The attempt to erase all the specifics of a culture aims to create a sense of timelessness. Whether writers are fully aware of it or not, they are showing contempt not just for the everyday, but for everyone now alive. They wish to be judged by posterity rather than their peers.

Second, in Britain, historical fiction has become so common that, if it was possible to speak of the judgement of posterity, the assumption would be that nothing of interest happened in the late twentieth and early twenty-first century. That is insane — if anything, we live in too exciting times.

Matt: The biggest problem with the predominance of historical fiction throughout the 1980s and 1990s (at least as far as reviews, prizes, and best-selling literary fiction) is that new, exciting voices have been marginalised. At the same time, readers have lost faith in literature. This balance needs to be redressed.

Nicholas: Current historical fiction seems to be written with the sole purpose of denying life. These novelists believe that literature belongs in a heritage theme park or, better, the grave. Anywhere but the here and now.

8 AS FAITHFUL REPRESENTATIONS OF THE PRESENT, OUR TEXTS WILL AVOID ALL IMPROBABLE OR UNKNOWABLE SPECULATION ABOUT THE PAST OR THE FUTURE.

Matt: This is the rule I like best. It seems like a comforting pact between the writer and the reader. It stops the writer weighting the odds. And it gives the characters a dignity that can be robbed by an omniscient narrator.

Nicholas: Absolutely. The bond between writer and reader is one of contemporaries, of peers, not master and initiate. Of course, there are readers who enjoy being patronised, but actually playing up to this slave mentality is shameful in a writer.

9 WE ARE MORALISTS, SO ALL TEXTS FEATURE A RECOGNISABLE ETHICAL REALITY.

Matt: We assumed this rule might cause more trouble than it eventually did. Apart from a few people quibbling over the difference between morals and ethics, no one seemed to worry about it. This rule seemed important because we wanted to highlight how contemporary fiction seems to have outgrown its interest in decadence. And hopefully this also means an end to the solipsism of the disco dads.

Nicholas: Dramas emerge out of recognisable situations: out of problems with relationships, the desires that bring friends into conflict, families into crises. So the idea that a novelist exists on a plane beyond contemporary ethics is unsupportable. It is a great source of regret to novelists that while visual artists can get away with turpentine-swilling moral turpitude, novelists are condemned to following respectable concerns. There are many, many writers who have embarrassed themselves by trying to keep pace with the myth of the degenerate artist. They should save themselves the effort. Artists are limited to making statements that carry their signature. Sometimes, their statements can change the world. But writers get to create entirely new ways for people to relate to each other, thus changing life itself. The writers' dependency on ethics ultimately affords the greater freedom.

10 NEVERTHELESS, OUR AIM IS INTEGRITY OF EXPRESSION, ABOVE AND BEYOND ANY COMMITMENT TO FORM.

Matt: We both had worries about using short stories as our medium rather than novels, especially as most criticism of short fiction tends to focus on whether the stories 'work', suggesting a kind of craftsmanship that interested us less than it might a more traditional editor. But this worry was assuaged by the fact that the rules make it harder to strive for an aesthetic 'perfection'. And this opens up a whole realm of different concerns and aesthetic choices and decisions.

Nicholas: Providing rules means that the stories were basically pre-edited. Once we had approached writers that we liked and, importantly, thought would be responsive to the New Puritan challenge, then so long as they respected the rules, we had virtually no editorial comments. And all the writers came up with something special. A poet once claimed that poets are the unacknowledged legislators, which they are clearly not. But fiction writers should at least be the ones who legislate what is and what is not fine writing. Which is what Rule 10 is about, the beyond-the-rules clause.

Matt: I'm not even sure it should be about 'fine' writing. The point is, everyone who looks at any of these stories can see immediately what makes them good and what makes them different. If this is a call to arms, then I feel we've got the right people.

Nicholas: Talking up a collection that includes one of your own stories verges on the egotistical. But the stories in this collection are so obviously both new and fantastic, I think it presents a real challenge to the critic to explain just why they work so well.

Mind Control

SCARLETT THOMAS

Mark got his Dreamcast five minutes before he died. His mother wanted it buried with him.

I've been living at Mark's parents' house since the day we first started going out together. And now he's dead, there doesn't seem to be any particular reason to move out. Mark's dad has become housebound. Mark's mother's bed-ridden. Me and Mark's dad take it in turns to take ice-cream up to her. Before the accident she only ate beetroot. Now she only eats ice-cream. I do all the shopping, because I'm the only one who goes out of the house.

Some things don't change. I'm still not allowed to cook garlic in the house, and they still put Diet Coke on the shopping list, even though they know I'll only put sugar in it. They still complain about how much I smoke. They still watch *The Bill* with me, although it's the only thing we ever do together. Mark's father still listens to '99 Red Balloons' once a day. I still do the housework for my keep. The only extra thing I do is rent Kevin Spacey films from the video shop for Mark's mother.

Oh, there is one more thing I do now. I water the plants. The garden here is huge. I don't see why the plants need to be watered at all. I'm sure that if they're genuinely suited to our climate they'll wait for it to rain. If not, they deserve to die. There's a hosepipe ban, so I fill a watering can from the tap by the house, and walk around the garden with it, every single night.

While I'm doing that, Mark's father talks to his fish. The fish pond is Mark's father's pride and joy The fish are all right-wing Christians, by the way. Or, at least, they must be after listening to the stuff Mark's dad plays to them on his short-wave radio. Thanks to whatshisname in Indiana, Mark's dad, the fish and me all know what to do in the event of the Second Coming, the coming of the anti-Christ, the rapture – whatever the hell that is – and where to buy seven years' worth of seeds for $198. Mark's dad is now convinced that the Columbine High School shootings were set up by the government. Me and the fish aren't sure.

Mark's dad has been thinking of buying a gun, lately, and a generator. He's not allowed to have the radio in the house, because of the Bristol Hum. Apparently, since 1976, Mark's mother has had this humming in her ears. It's not just her either, there are loads of people around here who have it. No one knows where it comes from, but it's like some kind of electrical sound, like a hairdryer a couple of rooms away. It drives some people mad. Some scientist suggested that it could be short-wave radio waves from Alaska, and Mark's mum was like, 'Get that thing out of here, and never bring it in again!' We tried to explain that the waves came from the sky and not from the radio, but maybe we were wrong, because the hum isn't bothering her so much now.

Tonight everything's pretty normal. I've hoovered most of the house, but not under any of the chairs, because it's not as if Mark's mother can check from her bed. I've polished the front of all the TV screens and cleaned both bathrooms. For dinner, Mark's mum has Chunky Monkey ice-cream. Me and Mark's dad have egg and chips, sitting in the lounge watching *Neighbours from Hell* in silence. Mark's dad only allows speaking during the commercial breaks, although it's hard to say anything with him complaining about all the ads.

Tonight there's one for sanitary towels.

'Flaming disgusting,' he says as usual.

I say nothing. I know better.

I've started doing experiments with the plants in the garden. I'm watering some of them with Evian, some of them with Somerfield sparkling peach spring water, some with tap water and some with nothing at all. The peach sample are now all dead, and I'm waiting to see which is the next least effective of the other watering methods. I'm so wrapped up in making notes in my book that I don't notice Mark's father lying prone by the fish pond.

When I eventually go to investigate, he seems to be out cold.

Whatshisname from Indiana is talking about Red China, where they burn bibles. During one particular bible-burning ceremony, the dirty communists didn't notice one brave Christian putting his hand into the flames and saving one single page of the Bible. It was this single page that was the basis of sermons for twenty years in that tiny community.

'The fish,' says Mark's dad, when he sits up.

I offer him some Evian. 'Are you OK?' I ask him.

'My fish,' he says, peering into the pond.

I look. There are no fish. Whatshisname cuts to some country-and-western Jesus song.

'Turn that rubbish off,' says Mark's father.

'I thought you liked it.'

'Not those flaming Jesus songs,' he says. 'Anyway, none of that matters any more. The only thing that matters is my fish. Where are they?'

We both look into the empty pond for five minutes. There are no fish. The plants must want their water, but they'll have to wait. Mark's father and I go back into the house.

'I'll get you a strong cup of tea,' I say.

Whichever way we look at it, the fish thing is weird. Mark's father is convinced that last night, while we were all asleep, some hooligans must have got over the back fence and taken them. I point out that hooligans wouldn't have bothered to catch all the fish, it's more likely that they just would have pissed in the pond or something. We rule out birds and decide the snatcher must be human. Nature isn't this exact. But even the human theory is problematic. Who would have had the patience to sit there until every single fish was caught? Surely human error would have left one or two fish?

'Specialists,' says Mark's father. 'Special nets.'

I think he might be losing it.

After I've tucked him up in bed, I sit up and think about it. Who would go to all the trouble of taking all the fish? Even when Mark's father feeds them, they don't all come up at once. His two favourites, Matthew and John, always tease him by hiding behind their algae until the last moment. If someone had fished for them, surely one or two of the clever ones would have had the sense to hide behind the algae like that as well?

'Poison,' I say the next morning over breakfast.

'Then where are the bodies?' says Mark's dad sadly.

'Acid, then,' I suggest. 'They could have dissolved.'

This is the first time I've ever seen Mark's dad cry.

'Dissolved,' he repeats.

'I could have put that better,' I say.

Then I take some Bailey's Haagen Daas up to Mark's mother. When I come back, Mark's father is flicking through a blank photo album.

For the next three weeks, fish is a touchy subject. We don't even have fish on a Friday now, which I'm quite pleased about, since it means I don't have to go to the fish and chip shop any more. I've had to give all our emergency tins of salmon to the old people's home down the road, and I have to censor the newspapers before Mark's father can read them. Luckily there's never much news about fish, but you can't ever be sure what they're going to have in the *Mail*.

The only fish story Mark's father was interested in seeing was the one the *Mail* didn't run, about his fish going missing. We spent a whole day compiling a fax to them and we both thought it had a good chance of being published, but nothing ever happened. Even Mark's dad's Christian fish, the one without the eye, has gone from the back of his Sierra. Not that he ever drives it, of course.

I've begun to take control of the short-wave radio, monitoring the Indiana output in case whatshisname starts talking about loaves and fishes, but he's too interested in gun laws right now, and water-purifying devices. The plants are suffering, because I hardly have time to water them. I just sit by the fishless pond with Mark's father for hours in silence, with my hand on the radio dial, just in case.

I think he sits there because he can't really believe they've gone. It's now been four weeks since they've gone, and he's still feeding them.

'Do you think you should stop feeding them now?' I suggest.

'They might still be in there,' he says.

'But the food's going mouldy on the top of the pond,' I say.

'They're hiding,' he says. 'They're scared.'

I'm really worried about him.

'They might just be invisible,' he suggests.

Recently, Mark's father has taken to going on the internet for long periods of time. I have to dial in for him and connect him to Yahoo. Once I've done that I'm not allowed into the computer room unless there are any technical problems. The computer room used to be the laundry. We don't do laundry any more.

While Mark's father surfs the internet looking for other people's experiences of missing fish, I continue to clean, take ice-cream to Mark's mother and play on the Dreamcast. I'm addicted to Shenmue, and the plants are suffering because of it. I don't get outside that much any more. Mark's father doesn't go outside at all. He doesn't even realise that he left his short-wave radio out there and it fell in the pond and went green. I'm wondering if I should fish it out in case he does ever go out there again. The pond's a pretty sad sight right now anyway. There's the rusty green radio, the mouldy food and the algae. The algae's grown a lot, probably because of all the water.

I wonder what Mark's father looks at on the internet. He says that apart from the missing fish searches, he only looks at the End Times website and other stuff recommended by whatshisname in Indiana. I never realised that through all those broadcasts, Mark's father was noting URLs in a little notebook, not knowing what URLs were, or even how to connect to the internet. He says that he was sure Jesus would eventually show him how to connect and then the URLs would come in handy.

Recently I suggested that we get another phone line, because of all the extra internet use. But when we dialled 1471 it said that the last person to phone us did so five weeks ago. So we probably don't need that line after all. Maybe if someone else dies we'll need to get one, but then people can always e-mail their condolences.

On the day I finish Shenmue, the fish come back. I run inside and tell Mark's father. He's praying to a website.

'Come quickly,' I tell him.

After some persuasion, he does.

It makes me feel nostalgic, us standing here looking at the pond like this. We stay here for at least two hours, talking about what's happened. I never knew how many fish there were in the first place, so I just assumed they had all come back. But Mark's father is absolutely positive that there are only half of them here. He knew he had exactly 110 fish. Now he says there are 55. I count. There are 55.

'John's there,' he says.

'Are you sure it's John?' I ask.

'Of course I'm sure.'

'What about Matthew?' I say.

'Not here. Gone.'

'Weird,' I say. 'Do you think someone returned half of them for a reason?'

'Who knows,' he says, rubbing his eyes. 'Who knows.'

Monaco

ALEX GARLAND

La Rascasse restaurant faces out onto the penultimate turn before the start/finish straight. I don't know what the food's like, but try getting a table over a race weekend – you'll find that Eurotrash beat you to the reservation by about twelve months.

A high fence protects the diners from flying tyres and suspension bars, in case of an accident. Men sit at tables and drink champagne, and girls stand pressed against the fence, with their fingers poking through. The men watch the girls. The girls have arms so slender that (if they could stand to risk such slender arms) they could reach through the chain links and touch the carbon fibre bodywork of the cars as they pass by.

Over the other side of the track, on the outside of the turn, there is a small grandstand. This, by contrast, is one of the least desirable spots to follow the Grand Prix. Here you see the Rascasse corner for what it is; a slow corner, with no real view of the cars' approach or retreat. The grandstand spectators won't see an overtaking move, unless it is the passing of a backmarker. They won't see a bounce over a chicane, or a feint left, or a jink right, or a late brake. Instead, they will see an unvarying procession of high-speed vehicles moving at a sluggish pace, and they will see the diners at Rascasse.

Finally, between La Rascasse and the grandstand, there is a narrow strip. No-man's land as far as the public is concerned, the strip runs the entire length of the Monaco circuit. It is there to service the race marshals and medics and fire crews and journalists. It also allows drivers who have crashed their ride to walk back to the paddock.

To stand here, you must first sign a piece of paper that says you take full responsibility for any harm that befalls you in this exposed position. Only an Armco barrier separates the strip from the track itself. Lean against the low metal guard, and be warned that if a car so much as clips the Armco the force of the vibration could break your ribs.

This is where I stood: a safe step from the Armco, my back to the grandstand, facing the track and La Rascasse.

La Rascasse. The guys watch the girls watch the cars pass by.

The guy was young, late twenties, blond, well-built, wearing a blue yachting blazer, and sitting at one of the most coveted tables, as close to the track as the restaurant could manage. The girl beside him was tall, brown-haired, and gold-skinned. She was maybe twenty-one or twenty-two, with a Spanish look about her. Her fingers poked through the chain-link fence.

A very pretty girl, exceptionally pretty even for young Eurotrash, so I raised my camera and started taking photos.

Using a fairly slow shutter speed, I was looking for a shot where she would be in focus, but the McLarens or Jordans passing a few feet in front of her would be a blur. The Saturday pre-qualifying practice session isn't good for much except picking up these local colour shots.

The girl saw me taking her picture. I zoomed in a little on her and she pouted outrageously and looked surprised. I took a few more pictures, zooming in further so that the cars were pretty much cut out of the frame. She squirmed and wriggled and showed me a full range of facial expressions. *Why are you taking my photo? Oh, I feel shy. Surely you don't think I'm so pretty? Oh, you do. Now I'm embarrassed. Now I'm angry. But I forgive you. Here's my smile.* She was as comfortable with a camera as that.

Stirling Moss would wave to pretty girls in pink lipstick as he controlled a four-wheel drift out of Casino Square. The four-wheel drift of Stirling Moss was a move that even Fangio envied. A beautiful thing, the lateral momentum of the car, kept from contact with the barriers not with the brake, but with the accelerator. The wheel turned in opposite lock, turned against the corner's natural direction. To drive a car that fast in that way is to be unnatural.

The girl's blond boyfriend saw the direction my camera was pointed, and he smiled too. He liked me taking photos of his girlfriend because that's what she was there for, and that's why he was sitting at Rascasse. He put down his wine glass – not champagne, I noticed blankly – and reached up to his girlfriend's white shirt. With an easy motion, his popped two of the buttons and tugged the shirt open, and a single tanned breast appeared.

I was momentarily flustered. Now I've *really* got a photo – flustered like that. I wondered if anyone else had noticed the girl's exposed breast and zoomed out the lens again, willing a car to pop into the frame.

Come on, I prayed. I need a car for this. I don't care who's driving it: for this girl, I need a streak of car in the frame.

But none appeared. Not even a lame Prost, not even a limping Minardi. The track was quiet and the pit-lane full.

Don't cover up, I prayed.

She didn't. Instead, without so much as a glance at her boyfriend, who was now looking up at her with quizzical amusement, the girl pulled open the other side of her shirt. Now with both her breasts fully exposed, she tilted her head provocatively and continued to gaze straight at my camera.

Not having much choice, I took a couple of shots of her and the empty road. But it was as good as useless next to the photo it could be.

No other photographers were elbowing beside me or jockeying for position because there were no other photographers. Nothing happens at Rascasse – we use the corner to leave the paddock and access the other parts of the circuit, where things *do* happen. The first corner, where cars crash; the opening of the tunnel, where cars flash into the shadowed entrance; the chiccane past the exit of the tunnel, where cars brake too late and bounce the kerbs or collide; the swimming pool, where the cars appear to be aiming directly at the camera lenses until – at the last moment – they jink right and then left into the short straight. The short straight that leads to Rascasse. Good for nothing but local colour.

The lower lip of the viewfinder was pressed hard into my cheekbone. The girl had undone the top button of her jeans and her smile had faded, replaced by a look of vague concentration. She slipped her left hand inside her waistband, her flies pulled open a little and, between her fingers, a neat stroke of dark hair appeared. The girl's knuckles began to move discreetly. I couldn't capture a movement like that on a camera. I had to concentrate on what I could capture.

In 1988, Ayrton Senna led the first sixty-six laps of Monaco, from pole position on the grid. On lap sixty-seven, he lost concentration just before the entrance of the tunnel and clipped the Armco, breaking no one's ribs but ending his race.

Monaco is unforgiving. Overtaking is nearly impossible, the slowest corner on the track can bring the cars to a near standstill. These cars are designed to drive fast, not crawl around sloping hairpins. Even the start/finish straight has a *curve* in it.

She's going to make herself come, I realised. I could see that from the tension that was forming around her mouth. And the boy, I think, could see it too, because he put his hand against the small of her back. For support or encouragement – it was the hand he had used to unbutton her shirt.

I wondered how many exposures I had left on my roll of film. There was no point switching to my back-up camera, because it had a wide-angle lens fitted and with the distance of the track between us, the girl and her flat brown stomach would as good as vanish.

So if I was to change lens, I might as well change film. But trying to jam in a new roll would be the interruption that snapped this elastic moment. If it wasn't the hurried motion, it would be the revelation that I had eyes behind the lens.

I guessed I had three shots left. Instinct, a thousand previously changed rolls, the internal clock and counting system that lets me set an alarm for seven thirty, and wakes me at seven twenty-five.

The girl, but no car.

Late May is when the F1 calendar hits Monaco. When the coastal sky is blue and cloudless, the May sun beats down hot enough to burn. That's why the older Eurotrash women have faces as cracked as Monte Carlo's harbour walls, wrinkles meshed around their eyes and mouths like the chain-link fences that protect them from flying tyres and suspension bars.

I could feel the sun on me. My T-shirt was stuck to my back and I could feel the strap of my camera bag shifting on my shoulder, sliding on the sweat.

The movement of the girl's knuckles had become less delicate and, although the direction of her gaze had remained steady, her focus on me was now indistinct. She used her free hand to widen the opening in her fly, and shifted on her feet, fractionally moving her legs further apart.

I took the first of my three remaining shots. In the corner of the frame, I caught the boyfriend at exactly the moment his eyes flicked in my direction.

The shutter reopened and the viewfinder cleared. The boy was looking at me with his eyebrows raised and one finger held up in the universal signal of pause. I don't know why, but the gesture made me hold my breath. A moment later, I heard the faint sound of an engine, accelerating. A car was leaving the pit-lane.

The boy's eyebrows raised higher, and his mouth spread

into a grin. Turning back to the girl, he said something to her or whispered something to her, and she responded, in kind, by biting her lower lip.

First lap out, taking it slow on the cool tyres, it would take over a minute and a half for the car to reach us.

The girl's mouth opened wide and she gasped. Then her hips bucked forwards once, in a prelude to her little death. A reflex action: all it took was a slight tightening of my grip on the camera, and I had accidentally taken the second of my three remaining photographs.

In France, they call it *petit mort*. Little death – everyone knows that. Eskimos have an infinite number of words for snow; if a butterfly flaps its wings then a hole appears in the ozone layer; when the French come they think they're dying.

Only two racers have died at Monaco. In 1952, Luigi Fagioli entered the tunnel in his Mercedes, but didn't come out the other side. Somewhere in the half-lit right-hand curve, he lost control, his tyres lost grip, he ran wide, he smashed into a stone balustrade. A decade and a half later, Lorenzo Bandini rolled his ride as he tried to negotiate the chicane. The car landed upside down on the straw bales that used to act as track barriers, and caught fire. Bandini was trapped and died later from his burns.

The accident happened on the eighty-first lap of a hundred-lap race. The following year, the Monaco circuit was reduced to eighty laps – as if it was the extra lap that had killed Bandini. Maybe it was, because no one has been killed since.

As the car left the tunnel, halfway around the circuit, thirty or so seconds away from where I stood, there was a sudden increase in the volume of the engine noise. The girl's hips bucked again and the boy looked back at me, and mouthed the make of the car.

From close by, the car engines sound like someone channelling an electric drill from your gut, up your neck, into your mind. Take your ear plugs out, and you'll lose balance. The noise will make you sway drunkenly on the heels of your feet and you'll reach out a hand to steady yourself.

Experts, *tifosi*, engineers and old hands – they can easily distinguish one car from another, just from the engine noise. But there is one engine that everybody knows. If you've heard it once, you will always recognise it if you hear it again. The engine noise is like a signature. I once heard an Italian journalist describe it as a machine gun firing through a vapour of blood.

The boy had mouthed 'Ferrari'. I heard the roar of the crowd in the grandstand behind me. They were calling out for the car that was coming, not the girl.

The Ferrari had exited the pit-lane and given a little burst on the accelerator up to the first corner, then turned right into the zig-zag ascent to Casino Square. Out of Casino Square and past the grandstand roar, the road dropped again, almost as steeply as it climbed. A hard brake into a hard right, and the Ferrari was coasting towards Lowes, Monaco's famous hairpin, the slowest corner on the Grand Prix calendar. Here, during a race, cars at the back of a pack will sometimes come to a standstill as they wait for the front-runners to clear the succession of slow turns that bring the circuit to the sea-front, and the tunnel.

In the tunnel, the Ferrari had opened up, putting a little heat in the tyres, rocketing past the concrete balustrades that had killed Fagioli.

Out of the tunnel, the engine noise had abruptly ripped across the harbour, then faded as the car slowed for the chicane.

Around the chicane, back on the power, passing the rows of multimillion-dollar yachts and their champagne deck parties.

Left, into the swimming pool complex.

Left again, the yachts here obscured by another grandstand.

Then right.

Then left.

Short burst on the power.

Slow, for . . .

Rascasse!

Stirling Moss used to wave at pretty girls in pink lipstick. But the driver of the Ferrari crashed.

Monaco is full of stories.

The first winner of the race, in 1929, was entered only as 'Williams'. Some legends describe him as a wealthy amateur, others as a humble chauffeur. But his real name was William Grover and he drove for the Bugatti team. Half-English, half-French, Grover enlisted as a driver in the Royal Army corps, where his bilingual ability led to him being recruited by Special Operations in 1942. He was trained as an undercover agent and parachuted back into France, where he landed near the Le Mans circuit. In Paris, he set up a sabotage network, and recruited two more racers, French drivers, Benoist and Wimille.

In 1943 the network was discovered. Grover was tortured by the Gestapo, then executed. Benoist escaped but was recaptured in 1944, and died at Buchenwald.

I don't know what happened to Wimille.

But I did get the photo.

The girl clutches at the fence with her free hand, head back, back arched. The boy half rises out of his seat. A diner looks towards the two of them as if he is only just comprehending what the girl has been doing. And another diner turns towards the foreground, where a Ferrari loses its back end in a cloud of burning rubber.

A Ghost Story (Director's Cut)

BEN RICHARDS

The train had arrived late on the outskirts of Preston and I felt a shiver of apprehension as I looked out at the darkness from the window. It wasn't just my dislike of arriving in Northern cities on Friday nights that made me edgy, although that was certainly a factor. More important, however, was my reluctance to leave the warmth and security of the train and to admit that the first stage of my flight had come to an end. I just wanted to stay suspended on the lightly swaying Virgin West-coast train, the other side of the dark, slow-moving, river Ribble. I didn't want to arrive anywhere but I certainly couldn't return.

The train shuddered and began to move again, pulling into Preston station. I looked for Martha from the window but couldn't see her. When I got off the train, she wasn't on the platform either and I felt a terrible panic, a hand at my throat. Other people were being met, lovers were kissing, parents and children were embracing, why wasn't she here?

'Jim,' a voice called from behind me. 'I'm over here. Have you gone blind?'

Fucking drama queen, a familiar voice muttered in my head.

'I got here rather early so I was having a coffee,' Martha said smiling as she walked towards me. 'The car's just out in the car park. Come on. I'm so happy to see you.'

Martha was one of my oldest friends. When I had been desperately casting around for somewhere to go, this had seemed the best option. In truth, it had been the only option. We had known each other from film school in Poland although Martha had long given up on the idea of making films. She was now a successful defence lawyer and was married to a TV producer called Gareth. Try as I might to find something against Gareth I really couldn't. He was generous, easy-going, good-natured. Somehow this still irritated me. I wondered whether he knew that Martha and I had slept together a couple of times a long time ago. It was not something that Martha and I ever talked about and I was glad – there was really nothing to say and we had managed to remain friends.

We drove out of the car park and through the dismal terraced suburbs of Preston, past a couple of dismal-looking men building up for a fight outside a pub. I craned my neck and was disappointed not to see the fight start. We left the town and crawled along impatiently behind a huge vehicle belonging to the local cement company, until we passed the British Aerospace factory at Salmesbury with its old jet plane perched outside the main gate.

'How's Juliana?' Martha asked me as we drove through the dark night into the Ribble Valley. 'That's all over then?'

'Yes. She said I was a neurotic, self-obsessed drama queen. That I interrupted her all the time and that when she did get a chance to speak I never listened.'

'Oh,' Martha said, glancing first at me and then in her rear-view mirror.

'Feel free to disagree with her,' I said.

'You've got lots of good points as well. I'm sure that Juliana would admit that.'

There was silence for a moment. 'And how have you been?' I asked.

'Well, things have been a bit . . .'

'I'm sorry, I just can't believe that anybody could say that I was self-obsessed!'

Martha looked at me sideways and laughed. 'There you are,' she said. 'At least you make jokes at your own expense. Not that that should always get you off the hook of course.'

'Well, it didn't,' I said. 'Did it?'

We were arriving in Clitheroe where Martha lived. It was not the sort of place I would ever have imagined for her. There was nothing wrong with it in itself – this wealthy market town with its pleasant, conservative inhabitants, its High Street of quality shops and good-value cafés running up to the castle. It just didn't really seem to me to suit the bright and lively girl I had known, the girl everybody had a crush on, the girl I had once written bad poems for. It did suit Gareth, who was originally from Burnley, and who made documentaries for a Leeds-based company about topics of contemporary concern such as the explosion of drug use among teenagers in rural villages.

One thing I did like about Clitheroe – that I had forgotten about from my previous visits – was the big fucker of a hill that lay behind it. Words like 'unfriendly' and 'moody' came to mind but these words were inappropriate because they were human qualities and there was nothing human about Pendle. 'Hill' seemed rather a little word for it as well. It was bestial and uncompromising, its rising dark ridge sharp across the night sky, its great flanks running down to the little towns and villages where bored teenagers were doing their utmost to get trashed. It was the place where the infamous Pendle witches were accused of cow-killing, milk-souring and general curse-laying before being taken to Lancaster jail and hanged. This was, of course, an act of great, misogynistic injustice etc. etc. but as I looked up at the hill I felt that a belief in witchcraft did not seem as unreasonable here as it might, say, in Kentish Town where I lived. The place was spooky enough now. It must have been even scarier a few centuries ago, illuminated only by candles and moonlight.

We pulled into the drive of Martha's house which was an old and elegant building just off the main road. A spotlight came on automatically as we went down the driveway and Martha swung the car around and into the garage. Once again, I didn't want to move, wanted to just stay in the car chatting to Martha. But each new stage had to be negotiated, I had to keep going.

'How are you, Jim?' Gareth held out his hand. It was a stupid question given that he knew perfectly well why I was there.

'So-so,' I said, trying to be upbeat as I moved piles of papers from a chair and sat down. A cat curled around my legs and I kicked it away.

'I shall have to get rid of these before Karen gets here tomorrow,' Martha murmured, straightening the papers.

'Who's Karen?' I asked, filled with dread at the prospect of another visitor besides myself.

'The cleaning lady,' Martha said, glancing at me.

I raised my eyebrows.

'I'm a working woman,' she said.

Gareth opened a bottle of wine and poured a glass for

himself and Martha. 'Orange juice? Diet Coke? Camomile tea?' Martha asked me.

'Normal tea,' I said. 'No, hold on, black coffee, please.'

'At this time of night? Decaff?'

I shrugged. It wouldn't make much difference.

After a while, they started to get ready for bed and I started to panic. Martha gave me a towel and showed me to the room I always slept in. She took my hand. 'Stay as long as you want,' she said. 'Goodnight, darling.'

I went and sat by the window, looking out at the bright stars and the dark shape of Pendle – a shape as massive, as intimidating as my loneliness. I looked at the pink towel on the chair, at the banal Monet print on the wall, at the stripy wallpaper, at the old-fashioned white wooden door with its latch, running at an odd angle against the low ceiling. The house smelt pleasantly of age, of use, but it was not my house. I was a stranger here, I was in the guest-room. I could hear low murmurs of conversation from Martha and Gareth's room. I hated Gareth. Self-satisfied northern cunt. Of course I didn't hate Gareth. He was not my enemy. Who was my enemy? Where were my numerous enemies? I took the towel and sniffed it and then I started to cry, looking at my crumpling face in the guest-mirror.

'How did you sleep?' Martha asked as we ate toast and marmalade the next morning.

'So-so,' I said, thinking how toast was always much nicer in somebody else's house. 'Fantastic toast. This toast is fucking delicious.'

Martha looked at me. 'I'm glad you like it,' she said evenly. 'Listen, Jim, I'll be back at about six, OK?'

'That's fine,' I said. 'Could you show me how to use the video, please?'

'Sure.'

When everybody had left the house, I padded about for a bit, looked in the various bedrooms, opened the drawers of Martha's desk, checked out the food cupboards, made myself a coffee. I studied the girls in short skirts arriving at the nearby grammar school. I felt strangely calm and went to the living room to watch a video. In spite of the débâcle over my film, it hadn't made me want to stop watching other people's work, quite the contrary. I wanted to understand, I needed to understand. I put a copy of *The Idiots* on and sat down on the large comfortable sofa. I had barely slept the night before and I found the film tedious so it was not long before I fell asleep and started a confused dream about witches. I awoke to find somebody shaking my arm. It was a girl. Her hair was almost in my face.

'Hey,' the girl said, 'you're missing your film.'

'Who the fucking hell are you?' I asked, scared.

'Charming.' She laughed. I rubbed my eyes and looked at her. She was wearing a short denim skirt, her legs were very white and there was a scab on her knee. She had long straight hair and was, I suppose, quite pretty. I guessed that she must be about twenty.

'I'm Karen,' she said. 'I'm the house-slave.'

'Martha said there was a cleaning-lady . . .'

'That's me.'

'I thought you'd be older. Cleaning-lady . . . it sounds . . .'

'Old. Yeah. What's the film?' She gestured at the screen. 'It's foreign.'

I explained about the Dogme movement and she wrinkled her nose.

'Sounds like they're right up their own arses,' she said cheerfully. 'Anyway, I think the director should get a credit.'

24

Too fucking right, Karen, I thought bitterly.

'Well, it's kind of anti the whole star-system thing. The idea of the director as *auteur*...'

'As what?'

'As *auteur*. You know, like the French ...'

'Oh,' she laughed. 'I thought you said otter. You know, like *Ring of Bright Water*? I loved that film when I was little. Do you want a cup of coffee?'

'Black, one sugar,' I said. I was starting to like Karen.

We sat and drank coffee and Karen told me about herself. She had just got back from Ibiza and was working to get some money to go away again. In the evenings, she served food in the local pub. She told me that the food was good, explained what they had on the menu, gossiped about her boss and the affair he was having with the bored wife of a local millionaire. It certainly wasn't very grim in this part of the north and I enjoyed listening to her. While I am not – admittedly – a very patient listener, certain voices have an almost hypnotic effect on me. Karen was a born story-teller, she had an utterly disarming frankness, a kind of self-contained quality and disregard for censure of which I felt envious. I care desperately about what people think about me, which is unfortunate because, on the whole, most people can't stand me.

'So, Martha says you've had sort of a nervous breakdown,' Karen said bluntly as the video clicked to an end and started rewinding. I hadn't seen any of it.

'Yeah, sort of.'

'Why?'

For some reason, I didn't mind her line of questioning at all. In fact, I found it rather refreshing. I suddenly remembered the feeling that I was walking on ice which was becoming thinner and thinner, the day when I had just crashed through into the freezing water.

'I don't know if there was just one thing really. I had spent some time in rehab because I'm an alcoholic. My girlfriend left me.'

'For another man?' Karen asked.

'She didn't need to leave me if she wanted other men. I think she just decided I was a prick, which is much more depressing.'

'I suppose it is,' Karen said.

'But I think the worst thing was my career. I'm a film director and the film I struggled for ages to make got made...' I tailed off.

'But that's good,' she said frowning. 'Your film got made, right?'

'Yeah, but it got no distribution, it just kind of died. If you don't get distribution – and unless you're prepared to kiss American arse you won't – you're fucked. I had put so much into that film.'

I remembered the whole process from development to screening, all the phone calls, the delays, the sudden moments of euphoria followed by raging anxiety attacks, the indifference which greeted its release, the total absence of phone calls from Los Angeles inviting me to come and pitch my next project. And the worst thing, the most painful thing, was that I had really expected these calls to happen because I believed that I had made a very good film.

'So what happened?' Karen asked.

'I went crazy and then I punched a film critic at a party.'

'Why did you punch him?' Her hand was at her mouth, she was listening intently.

'Because he wrote a really snidey review saying that I was a failed magic realist. Ignorant bastard. I don't mind bad reviews...' (this was, of course, totally untrue) '...but I can't stand it when some lazy, jumped-up public-school wanker just misses the point completely. IT WAS A SATIRE!' I thumped the arm of the sofa a little too vehemently. I remembered my toast outburst and resolved to calm down.

'Oh well,' Karen said, 'you were probably right to punch him then.'

'He might take me to court. I didn't just punch him once.' I remembered his bulging terrified eyes as my hands tightened around his throat and I tried to get his ear into my mouth so that I could bite it off. I remembered a woman screaming and people trying to drag me off him. 'It was kind of pathetic,' I admitted.

'It always is,' Karen leaned on the Hoover. 'If I had a nervous breakdown every time I made a twat of myself, I'd be hoovering in a straitjacket.' She folded her arms across her chest and pushed the Hoover along with her forearms and grinned.

'I'll never make another film,' I said.

'Yeah, you will. If you're really a film-maker then you won't be able to stop yourself. Anyway, count yourself lucky. At least your film got made.'

She wasn't the first person to say this to me.

'So, did Karen disturb you?' Martha asked that evening over dinner. I had promised to cook and so we were eating pasta with a tub of Sainsbury's tomato and mascarpone sauce. Gareth was working down in London.

'No,' I said. 'I really liked her. We talked about film theory.'

'Did you?' Martha asked doubtfully. 'I thought she was just into pills and casual sex.'

'As opposed to formal sex?' I was slightly irritated by her tone. 'Perhaps Gareth should make a documentary about her,' I added sharply. Then I relented because it was Martha, my best friend, my learned friend, one of the few people I could truthfully say that I loved. I changed the subject. 'Pasta shells are far superior to bows or spirals, aren't they? They tend to hold sauce much better in my opinion.'

'I've never really given it much thought,' Martha said. 'By the way, I think I'd better let you know as you'll probably get wind of it soon enough. I'm pregnant.'

'Oh right,' I said flatly.

'Congratulations, Martha,' Martha said. 'I'm so happy for you. Can I be a god-parent?'

'Well, it's great news,' I said.

She laughed. 'I need some of my friends to think that it's not good news. So you don't need to pretend. I was positively looking forward to the expression on your face, and you know what?'

'What?' I said.

'You didn't let me down. Come on, let's wash up.'

That night Martha came to my room. She was wearing white pyjamas.

'We can't have sex,' I said. 'I'm mad and you're pregnant.'

'I don't want to have sex with you,' she said, padding over and getting under the covers. 'Frankly, it was no great event the first time round.'

'That's good,' I said. 'Because I find pregnant women a total turn-off.'

We both laughed. She snuggled up against me, rubbing her cold feet on my ankles. One of her curls tickled my nose. 'I don't love Gareth,' she whispered in my ear and then we fell asleep. When I awoke in the morning she wasn't there and I wondered whether I had dreamed the whole thing.

Over the next couple of weeks I watched videos and spent a lot of time in the company of Karen. Sometimes, in between her cleaning and leaving to serve in the pub, we watched videos together. She would bring bags from Blockbusters to the house. Our combined taste was eclectic. We watched *Festen* and agreed that it was better than *The Idiots*. Of course, we had our differences. She liked Scorsese while I thought he was overrated – especially *GoodFellas*. Karen refused to watch any sci-fi films which she hated passionately. In fact, she was rather dogmatic about anything containing special effects so horror films were out as well. We had agreed on a right to veto and Karen blocked *Starship Troopers*. I disliked romantic comedies and used my veto accordingly. This led to a row about *Sliding Doors* on which I applied a double-veto because it had Gwyneth Paltrow in it. In the end I had to compromise and watch a Meg Ryan romantic comedy which I slagged off but secretly quite enjoyed. We watched *Bringing up Baby*, *(William Shakespeare's) Romeo and Juliet*, *The Third Man*, *Anaconda*, *Wild Strawberries*, *Titanic*.

'Kate Winslet's got fantastic tits,' Karen observed during the scene where Kate was being painted by Leonardo di Caprio.

Karen, I had discovered, was utterly uninhibited on the subject of sex. She chatted cheerfully away about what she and her friend Jane had got up to in Ibiza.

'I had a kind of tick-list', she said while we were fast-forwarding from Kate's breasts to iceberg, sinking etc., 'of things I wanted to do and I did most of them.'

I listened enviously while she recounted her exploits and didn't mention my own tick-list which although long had worryingly few ticks on it. At night I would use some of her stories as the basis for explicit and disturbing sexual fantasies although I was never the protagonist, nor even an actor (of course!) and during the day I felt no sexual desire for her whatsoever.

She sang while she cleaned. I would hear her around the house trilling a curious repertoire of pop and traditional songs. Bob Marley's 'Three Little Birds' or 'My Bonnie Lies over the Ocean'. But what I liked most was listening to her disarmingly honest stories. Sometimes, she would get so involved in them that she would perform actions as well. Once she even threw herself on the floor when describing a fight she had seen.

'I had a parrot in Ibiza,' she told me once. 'Custard. I loved that parrot. She had a little diamanté collar and she talked. Well, actually, she could only say one word . . .'

'What was that?' I asked.

'Balloon,' she said, frowning. 'Fuck knows where she got that from. Anyway, one day Custard disappeared.'

'Escaped?'

'Stolen. She was on my balcony and some fucking gypsies stole her. I put signs up everywhere, I even offered a reward. I heard rumours that the gypsies had sold Custard and I offered to buy her back. Nothing . . .' She paused and shook her head.

'Too bad,' I said sympathetically.

She held her hand up sternly to show that she had not finished. 'One night I was off my face. I was totally spannered. I went with my mate Middlesbrough Dave to this tranny bar. He's a right fucking lunatic – got two years for dealing. Anyway, I walk in, right, and behind the bar in a cage all decorated with fairy lights, still wearing the collar I bought her was . . . guess who?'

'Margaret Thatcher,' I said.

Karen frowned. She did not like facetious humour.

'Custard. I knew it was her 'cause of the collar and when she saw me she started shrieking "balloon, balloon, balloon". The gyppoes had sold her to the trannies.'

'Bastards. So did you take her back?'

'Nah. She was happy there. She was a star. The trannies fucking loved her, of course. I thought about it but I didn't want to take her on a plane anyway and I had to come back here for a while.'

'Where are you going next?'

'I dunno. Somewhere where there's no blokes in football shirts. I hate that, you know. The way they walk down the streets in foreign countries in their football shirts like they own the place, their skin all red, their stupid expressions. Do you want a cup of coffee? Then I thought we could watch this.'

She took out a copy of *Happiness*. I had seen it in the cinema but didn't mind watching it again. As she kneeled down to put it in the machine, she said to me, 'You're not a prick really.'

'What?' I said, surprised.

'Your girlfriend was wrong. You're not a prick. Don't be so hard on yourself. You're a good person to watch films with.'

'Thanks,' I said.

'You're welcome,' she replied.

One day I got up as usual and went through my usual routines of making myself coffee, snooping through any personal stuff I could find, reading for a little bit. That day Karen did not appear and I was annoyed and had to watch *Notting Hill* on my own. After a while I couldn't take any more Hugh Grant so I went to the window and watched the sixth-form girls smoking at the bus stop and felt old.

The next morning at breakfast I noticed that Martha was troubled and knew immediately that something was wrong.

'There's been an accident,' she told me. My head began to spin.

That evening on the local news, we saw the car all crumpled and burned where it had hit a wall and caught fire. There was considerable tut-tutting about the fact that there had been six young people in such a small vehicle and that all of the occupants had consumed such large quantities of alcohol and drugs. Nevertheless, everybody agreed that it was a tragedy. There were interviews with the drug tsar who said that it was a terrible waste of young lives but that hopefully it would serve as a lesson. I longed for a bolt of lightning to streak down and split him in half.

'Are you OK?' Martha asked me. 'I know you got on very well.'

'I'm OK,' I said, glancing at the place on the sofa where Karen had sat in her short denim skirt, one long white leg crossed over the other, picking at her scab absentmindedly. 'It wasn't like I'd known her for years or anything.'

But I couldn't stay in the living room any longer. I went upstairs and looked out of my window and rubbed my eyes. Above the town was Pendle, although it looked relatively benign on this early spring morning, not as dark and foreboding as the night I had arrived. I remembered Karen singing 'My bonnie lies over the ocean'. I thought about the way in which she led her life – moving about always, her easy attitude to work and sex and drugs, how she had shrieked with laughter at certain points in films, the way she seemed somehow unencumbered.

I sat, looking out of the window and suddenly saw myself, terrified and unhappy, on the train which had stopped just outside Preston. I remembered the soft tickle of Martha's hair as she lay beside me and whispered her secret in my ear. Something was happening in my mind, in my mind's eye, something was stirring, shifting, stretching. I stood up, half-agitated, began to pace the room. Because these images were giving rise to new images and when I thought about that burning car I knew that I was seeing more than the sad and untimely death of a girl of whom I had grown very fond. I was seeing the blazing wreck repeated and reflected on the eyeballs of popcorn-crunching spectators – little licks of light in the darkness of the stalls.

Was this yet another example of my egotism, my self-obsession? Did it make me Gareth, who I knew was itching to use the image of the burned-out car in his documentary on the perils of drug-taking among teenagers in rural villages? Perhaps. Perhaps. But I did not just imagine the burning car accompanied by a sombre commentary and an interview with the drug tsar. I saw a girl in an imaginary straitjacket grinning as she pushed a Hoover with her forearms, I heard a cheerful voice singing 'Bring back, bring back'. And I saw a parrot in a diamanté collar, squawking in recognition from its cage garlanded with fairy lights.

Short Guide to Game Theory

NICHOLAS BLINCOE

The object of SWING™ is to create and market a pop group. A pack of cards defines potential band members as the loud one, the pierced-and-tattooed one, the virgin, and so on. Players pick up cards as they move around the board. Once they have a set of five different cards, they look for a record deal, play a festival, release a single. Simple. I return the board and the cards to the padded envelope and begin to read the designer's letter.

Dear Sir,

Please find enclosed your required SAE and cheque for fifty pounds. Also the counters, cards and board for the game SWING™ and this letter, which includes the rules of the game on the attached ten sheets.

yours sincerely

Duncan Taverner

Everyone who submits a game to our company includes a cheque for fifty pounds. This is for administration purposes, but we do provide a professional evaluation of all games received. Fifty pounds is about average for a reputable games developer. Of our biggest competitors, Games Talk, charge a little less, Cactus Marketing a little more. At some point, I am going to have to write to Duncan Taverner and explain why SWING™ is unmarketable. The problem is that I know him. He was my best friend for about three months, aged eleven or twelve. It is definitely the same Duncan Taverner, the address on the SAE is only half a mile from his parents' house in Bristol, our home town.

I cannot face writing Duncan's rejection letter yet so I go through my post, focusing on the smaller envelopes rather than the big packages. Most of these letters contain confidentiality agreements. More and more prospective designers ask us to sign agreements before sending their games for evaluation. If the wording is acceptable, I sign. If it isn't, I suggest any extra clause we might require. When I first began working as a games developer, I assumed there would be a legal department to handle questions like this. But it is pretty straightforward.

After lunch, I decide to write Duncan a personal letter rather than use the more formal rejection / analysis document stored on my computer. I remind him of the games we played as kids, games with themes about making films, or managing football teams or simply becoming a millionaire. All were similar to Monopoly and worked on the assumption that, as Monopoly was a role-playing game, other roles could be substituted. The truth, though, is that no one ever plays Monopoly to fantasise about being a property developer. As I tell Duncan, it is the feel of the game, the way that it plays, that makes Monopoly so compelling. It tantalises by keeping hopes alive, round after round, until it finally delivers a clear winner and one or more definite losers. Waddingtons hit the perfect note with Monopoly. The rip-offs never lasted more than a season and the arrival of the video game killed them off for good. I mention Championship Manager as a kind of modern classic which works better as an electronic game than it ever could as a boardgame. I sign off with a matey 'All the best, Dan' and then tag on a P.S. suggesting that Duncan learns programming and develops SWING™ for the Sony PlayStation.

After five minutes, I reopen the envelope and add a P.P.S., the way kids do in their letters. I say that whether SWING™ is a boardgame or a video game, I bet I would still beat him at it, every time.

On Wednesday I get a fax.

Daniel, you turd. I read your patronising letter and you can stick it up your arse. SWING™ is nothing like Monopoly. I do not want to play a Sony fucking PlayStation. I want a game where I interact with humans and compete skill-for-skill in a music business experience. If I wanted to mong in front of the box, then I would get a Sony PlayStation. But then I might turn out like you. Obviously you do not understand my game. Well, maybe you are new in your job. Maybe you will learn. But I will get my game made through another company. So fuck off.

Yours Duncan Taverner.

P.S. I hated playing boardgames with you when we

were kids because you were such a smug tosser. You have not changed.

P.P.S. Give me my fifty quid back, dickhead.

I send Duncan fifty quid out of my own pocket. I do not want to explain what happened to my boss, which I would have to do before I can refund the money through the company.

At the weekend, I am supposed to go to a games conference at the University of Warwick. The organisers have asked me to hold a series of clinics for aspiring designers. Now I worry that Duncan Taverner will turn up and everything will get unpleasant. But then I think of all the people who might recognise my name from old rejection letters. If I am comfortable meeting them, I shouldn't be nervous about Duncan Taverner. Until this moment, I was actually looking forward to the conference: drinking, partying, catching up on gossip with people from within the industry.

When I arrive on the university campus, I am given a modernist split-level room with an en suite bathroom and an assurance that only other developers are in this building. The designers have been put in different halls of residence with much worse amenities. It is the Easter break so there are no students around, just a variety of conferences ranging from the travel industry, through insurance services to Gaming 2000.

I am very impressed with my room. It reminds me of something out of the film *The Ice Storm*, with its enormous double-height windows and the flight of hardwood steps that lead to an upper gallery level. The gallery is small, just enough room for two single beds, but the beds face the window and beyond the gallery rail there is a sweeping view of the Warwickshire countryside. I haul my suitcase up to the gallery, swing it on to the nearest bed and then go downstairs. I sit on the sofa and stare out of the window until long after it gets dark. At eight-thirty, I visit a bar called the Airport Lounge for the conference's meet-and-greet session. The woman at the front table hands me a badge with my name on it. I take a few moments to put it on, casually looking over the other badges arranged in alphabetical order on the table-top. I feel quite disturbed when I see a badge for Duncan Taverner lying there, unclaimed. At least it means he is not here yet. I wonder what to do.

I end up drinking eight pints of lager and singing 'The Name of the Game' with sixty amateur games designers, a woman called Jessica from my company and a group of rival developers. Then I have fish and chips from a polystyrene box. I don't see Duncan but I notice that his badge has disappeared by the end of the night.

I have fish and chips again for breakfast. They leave my lips feeling greasy so I go and wash and then find I am late for my ten o'clock meeting. I am supposed to go to room SO 102 in the Social Studies block. When I finally arrive, I apologise, but the man waiting at the little table tells me it does not matter. He has already set out his game board, which resembles Monopoly except that instead of hats, irons and ships, it has little microphone stands.

I say, 'Hello. What's this then?'

He shushes me. 'First things first, mate. Sign this.'

He gives me a confidentiality agreement, printed out on a dot matrix printer. The wording is absolutely standard and I am happy to sign. But first I ask, 'Is this a music business game?'

'I am not prepared to say at this moment. Sign the form.'

I hand back the signed agreement. 'It is a music business game, isn't it?'

He shifts in his seat. 'The game is called Boy Zone. The object is to successfully manage the group Boy Zone, taking them to world pop domination.'

The game is virtually identical to Duncan Taverner's game, which isn't a surprise in itself. After a couple of rounds, I explain that the game-playing is much too conventional. For a new game to succeed in the current marketplace, there has to be an unusual and distinctive element. The designer nods and asks whether I think Ronan Keating might provide development funding. He says that his job running the family plumbing business does not leave him enough time to really concentrate on the game. I tell him it won't hurt to ask.

My second appointment is also in the Social Studies block. This time I am early, partly because I have left the Boy Zone man before his hour was up and partly because I have now figured out the room numbering system used in the Social Studies department. But again, the designer is there before me. She says, 'Mr Thomas?'

'That's right. Do you want to sit down, we'll get cracking on your game.'

'Would you mind signing this first?'

She also has a confidentiality agreement. The combination of Tippex blobs and jumpy type makes it look like an historical artefact. You just don't see typewritten documents any more. But the wording is fine. I take out my biro and sign, laughing as I ask her, 'This isn't a music game, is it?'

Her eyes narrow. 'It's called Pop Starz, a game for all the family.'

I feel uncomfortable throughout the entire session. I really shouldn't. I keep telling myself it's a perfectly likely coincidence. But I am glad when the hour is up. On the way to my next appointment, I bump into another developer. We stand and gossip for a few minutes as we drink tea from a big urn. He is on his way to give a lecture on the future of Trivia games, which I am sorry to miss. We arrange to have a beer later.

My twelve o'clock appointment shows me a game called Heavy Metal Holocaust – the game that rocks.

The University of Warwick has an Arts Centre with a theatre and cinema and a bar that sells sandwiches. I have a packet of crisps because there are only cheese sandwiches left and I am lactose intolerant. I could go somewhere else to eat but I have been traipsing all over the campus looking for Duncan. The Arts Centre is the last place I look. He is leaning against the bar's melamine wood-look surface. I say, 'Hello. Are we talking?'

'Do I know you, mate?'

'Come on, Duncan. It's me, Dan Thomas.'

'Oh.' He sips his pint, holding cold eyes steady on me.

I am almost positive he has orchestrated the whole glut of music biz games. But I don't want to get into a shouting match, so I begin by apologising. I tell him that when I sent him the letter about his game, I was trying to be casual. I tell him that I see now, I probably came across as a bit of a smart arse.

'Yeah. Well.' He takes another sip. 'Maybe you're new in the job. I don't know.'

'I've been doing it five years.'

'Five years? I've been working on different games for fifteen years. So I think I know what I am talking about.'

We are both twenty-six years old, so Duncan must have been trying to invent a game since we were friends. I say, 'I'm sorry. I was out of order.' Then I try a subtle line, hoping to test him out. 'You have to realise, it's a very competitive field. And the music business is a popular subject, you're up against all the other people trying to develop a game.'

Duncan says, 'Are there other music business games?'

He's playing it so well, I am beginning to doubt myself. Maybe it is just a coincidence that every game I see has a music theme. So I just tell him, 'I've seen a few.'

'Like what?'

'You know, moving around a board, collecting musicians and releasing hit singles. That kind of thing.'

He almost drops his pint. 'That's the concept behind SWING™'

His reaction seems so genuine, I am getting more and more uncomfortable. I want to change the subject, so I ask if I can get him another drink.

He ignores me. 'What are their games like?' He is practically shouting.

Our conversation is going so badly, I am looking for a way to close the whole topic. I think I see a way out. I apologise again. 'I can't tell you, Duncan. When they show me their games, I sign a confidentiality agreement.'

He stops. His mouth is open, his eyes flickering. 'You never signed a confidentiality agreement about my game.'

It's true, I didn't. He never asked me to.

'So you can tell them all about my game, but you can't tell me anything about theirs?'

'That isn't the way we work, Duncan. I wouldn't tell anyone about your game.'

'What's stopping you? You never signed anything, you

can screw me over any time you feel like it.'

'I wouldn't do that. It's not the way we work.' I don't
know what else to say. I don't want to tell him that I would
never screw over a mate, because that would only make him
more wary. So I just look at my watch and say, 'Christ, is
that the time.'

My one o'clock meeting is in room SO 204. I am out of
breath from running and more than fifteen minutes early. I
smoke a cigarette and stand staring out of the office window
at a pretty square below. There are vines covering wooden
frames. Beneath them, games developers stand talking in
groups of two and three. Games developers do not
necessarily look similar, but they tend to walk around with
boardgames under their arms.

At one o' clock exactly, a man walks in and introduces
himself as Harry Thorpe. After asking me to sign a
confidentiality agreement, Harry spreads a deck of cards out
on the table.

'OK. Fifty-two cards in four suits: Mitsubishi, Dog Bone,
Fork and No U-Turn.' Harry holds up a card in turn as he
tells me its name. I nod. I am just relieved that the cards
have nothing to do with music, so far.

'The face cards are Bette Davis, Elvis Presley and Jack
Duckworth of *Coronation Street* fame. Last of all, there is a
Polo card.'

I look at a card with a picture of a Polo mint in the
middle. Harry looks at me expectantly, so I nod again. So
far, everything is fine. I am following him.

After shuffling the deck, Harry deals us five cards each,
face down on the table.

'Should I look, Harry?'

He shakes his head. 'First, you have to put in a token.'

'Like an ante?'

'If you like.'

I throw in my ante and look at my cards. I have a pair of Jacks. I tell Harry that I'll open and put two extra tokens on the table in front of me.

'You catch on fast,' Harry says. 'I'll call.'

I get rid of three cards and draw a pair of Polo mints. A very good hand. I say, 'You sent me this game for evaluation, Harry. Didn't you get my analysis?'

'Was that you? Daniel Thomas? I thought what you said was very interesting. I've made a few changes and I thought I would see how it plays in a real competitive situation.'

It is true. He has made changes. We are playing Five-Card Draw. When he sent me the game a month ago, he enclosed the rules for Stud poker with it.

'I think it plays very well, Harry. Though it would work better with five to seven players.'

'Well, you're the one with the experience. I dare say you know what you're talking about.'

He draws two cards. I check. He raises me so I call. He beats my two pairs with a Straight Flush: five, six, seven, eight and nine of Mitsubishi. I assume that he has cheated. But I say, 'Nice hand, Harry. I'll catch you later.'

I couldn't tell whether Harry was a nut or not. But I enjoyed the game and by the time I reach my three o'clock meeting I am feeling much more relaxed. The designer is already waiting for me, nervously flapping a confidentiality agreement. It is the first time I have seen one written in crayon. The wording is all over the place but I sign it anyway. I don't want to suggest any changes because I am afraid the man might burst into tears. Then he pulls out his game. It is called SPICE WORLD.

I don't care how timid the man looks. I will not be fucked

with. I prod him in the chest. 'Is this supposed to be funny?'

He almost collapses. It seems to take for ever before he stops hyperventilating and stammers out the words: 'It's not supposed to be funny. It's a game based on Ginger and Baby Spice, the most interesting of the Spice girls.'

'OK.' I squint down at the man. I can't believe anyone could have singled out those two as his favourite pair. I can only assume he has a Madonna-Whore complex. What I don't know is whether he is dangerous or not. I look around the room, wondering whether Duncan Taverner is hiding in a cupboard for a joke. But there is no cupboard. I say, 'OK. Talk me through it.'

The game isn't at all what I expected. After less than ten minutes' playing time, I am hooked. It is a game for two people with an abstract board, like draughts or even the Chinese game Go, rather than the more naturalistic boards used in contemporary games. One player takes the red Geri Halliwell counters and the other the white Emma Bunton counters. Geri moves first, making reckless plays as she advances quickly across the board. The Emma character has to play defensively, using more rational strategies. The object of the game is to make it impossible for the other player to move. In Geri's case, this happens when her counters are scattered uselessly across the board. In Emma's case, it happens when she is too hemmed in to break out of Geri's grip.

After three quarters of an hour, I say, 'This is very good. My only real suggestion would be to break with the Spice Girl theme.'

'Why would I want to do that?'

'Well, for one thing, the time for a *Spice World* movie tie-in is probably long passed. And for another, Geri left the Spice Girls two years ago.'

'I know that.' He looks at me as though I am the weirdo. 'The game reflects Emma and Geri's struggle to dominate the hit parade with their solo singles in November 1999.'

I give him my card. 'Let's talk next week. I think you might have something here.'

After the Airport Lounge bar shuts, I end up playing poker around a table in a student kitchen on the other side of the campus.

Besides myself and Harry Thorpe, there is Jessica from my company and four guys from the rival companies. I am doing quite well, careful never to bet against Harry, who is an incredible cheat. I never actually see him do anything – I just know that it is impossible to get the kind of hands he is dealing himself. The odds against drawing Four of a Kind are around 4,000 to one. Harry gets one an hour: first getting sixes with a Polo as his fifth card, then four Elvis Presley's and a Bette Davis.

One of the other guys asks, 'Why have you called the suits Dog Bone and No U-Turn?'

Harry says, 'That's for the kiddies.'

Harry has laid on a couple of bottles of Jim Beam, which is a good idea. If his opponents are drunk, there is less chance of them realising they are being robbed. Jessica is pretty far gone. She is complaining about her day, saying, 'Can you believe the level of games we are getting here?'

One of the other men says, 'Check this out, I got four different ideas for football games. You believe that? Four in one day.'

Everyone nods, including me. I know it is possible. At one conference I went to, I saw three dinosaur games in one afternoon. I realise now that I was being paranoid, imagining that Duncan Taverner had organised all those music games to freak me out. But even so, I ask if anyone else has seen any games with a pop theme.

Jessica answers first, shaking her head and calling me at the same time. She puts another two pound coins on the table. My question is passed around the table, everyone shaking their heads and either calling or throwing in their hand.

Harry wins on the showdown with Three of a Kind. The odds are around 250 to one against.

I say, 'I have to go.' I guess I am thirty quid up. Everyone else is down by between twenty and a hundred pounds. Harry has won at least £200 and is going to win a lot more if the others don't have the sense to go to bed. I have a feeling the men will play for as long as Jessica sits at the table. There is that kind of vibe. I am convinced Harry planned it that way, inviting Jessica deliberately. He is careful never to take money from her – that was left to me. I give Harry a discreet little salute as I leave the room: I recognise a winner when I see one.

My room looks so peaceful, flooded with silver-grey moonlight. In front of me, long white curtains billow against the double-height windows. As I flick on the light, the windows are transformed into a huge mirror. I see a reflection swoop down. It might be a ghost or even a kind of wild animal. As the body lands on top of me, I realise it is Duncan Taverner. He was lying in wait for me, perched on the rail around the gallery.

'You twat. Make a fucking fool out of me.' He is winded but not as winded as me. I am bent double on the floor trying to catch my breath and wondering whether Duncan broke my collarbone as he landed on me.

Then he boots me in the ribs.

'Ow. You bastard.' I forget about my shoulder and

scrabble across the floor, trying to get behind the sofa so he cannot kick me again. 'What the hell are you playing at?'

'Like you don't know.' He is shouting. 'You don't think it's suspicious that every other person has a music game?'

He throws a waste-paper basket at me. I dodge. I need to plan a counter-attack, otherwise he is really going to do me some damage. He is getting ready to strike again, shifting his weight onto his forward foot, holding a desk lamp in his hand. I run for the stairs to the gallery. Duncan goes for my ankles, missing by about five centimetres.

Once I am up there, I haul the mattress off my bed and block the top of the stairs. With my body weight against it, there is no way Duncan can get past. I peer round the edge of the mattress, looking under the safety rail and down to the rest of the room. Duncan leaps up and almost punches me in the head. But then when he tries to grab hold of the underside of the gallery and haul himself up, I swing a foot around and boot him off. It is stalemate.

He rubs his head, saying, 'You can't stay up there for ever.'

'It's my room. Where else am I going to go?' My back to the mattress, I am panting hard. I say, 'What about I sign a confidentiality agreement now.'

'It's too late for that. You've already told everyone.'

'I haven't told anyone, you moron.' I regret calling him a moron almost immediately. I try to soften my voice. 'You know what I thought when I saw all those music games? I thought you had arranged the whole thing, just to get your own back on me.'

Duncan says, 'That's always your problem — thinking people are playing games with you.'

I cannot see him, but I sense him down there: a dark, dense figure. He is right about me though.

He says, 'I only used to play those boardgames with you for a laugh. You spoiled them all. You always reckoned I had these devious strategies, but I didn't.'

'You were so good, you must have had strategies.'

'Bollocks. If you really thought I was so super-intelligent, why was I so easy to beat?'

'Because I always cheated.' I know he is shocked. I try to think of something to say. The best thing I can come up with is, 'You could have cheated too. It was your choice.'

I know it is no argument. I imagine I am going to be sitting up here for a long time yet. I am tired and I am hungry. The only thing I have to eat is a bar of chocolate and if I eat more than two pieces, my lactose intolerance will kick in and I'll have to go to the toilet. I am in a very difficult position.

Down below, Duncan is saying, 'Bastard, bastard, bastard.' But he is saying it to himself, just whispering it over and over.

I peer around the mattress again. Duncan is sitting on the sofa below, his head in his hands. I think he is crying. I say, 'I am going to come down, Duncan. If you hit me again, well, there's nothing I can do about it. But afterwards, I will call the cops or something.'

Duncan doesn't reply. I can see his shoulders shivering as he sobs. I hate seeing him like that.

'I can help you with your game. We'll make it a real success, Duncan.'

Monday morning after the conference, I phone in sick. Duncan watches me put down the receiver. He now thinks of me as a cheat, so it is no surprise to him that I lie so well on the telephone. It is not really a lie, anyway. Apart from anything, my bruises make it uncomfortable to move around. I pop my toast out of the toaster and offer Duncan another cup of coffee.

He shakes his head. He only has one thing on his mind. I know I am going to have to give him my pitch. And it needs to be strong. I point a finger of toast at him. 'Your problem, Duncan, you think you like games. But how many do you actually play? Monopoly. Maybe Scrabble or Trivial Pursuits when you've invited friends around. And you think there's room for a new game. There isn't. And definitely not SWING™. It is boring, old-fashioned and plays worse than the games it is ripping off.'

'I wanted it to be old-fashioned. A nice old-fashioned game.'

I hope he isn't going to start crying again. He is staring down at the lino, hiding his face.

'Listen Duncan. When something is old-fashioned, it means no one is interested in it any more. If they were it would have stayed in fashion.'

'And you really think SWING™ would work better as a strategy game for two players?'

'It's the essence of music. It's all about creative differences: Jagger and Richards, Lennon and McCartney.'

'They write songs together. They don't fight each other.'

'Well, the Gallagher brothers, then. Or Mark E. Smith and the rest of the Fall.' I almost say Shaun Ryder and the Happy Mondays but I realise that all my examples are from Manchester. 'Or, you know, Ike and Tina.'

He doesn't look convinced.

'It's about friendship, Duncan. You have one character who is always pulling stunts, and another who has to absorb all the shit. That's what this game is about. A strategy game where one player is deliberately reckless and the other is cautious and rational. It will be a classic, believe me.'

I think about the man with his Spice Girl game and his confidentiality agreement. It isn't worth the crayon it was written with. I hope.

'OK,' Duncan says. He takes a seat, squaring up to the board I've set up on my kitchen table. 'I'll take the red counters.'

'Will you fuck, Duncan.' I push the white counters his way.

'Let's not run before you can walk.'

Mr Miller

CANDIDA CLARK

The place is steaming. Damp bodies, infernal smoke and eddies of congealed air fester in the corners of the bar. Everyone looks glum. So when Mr Miller storms in here, all eyes are instantly upon him, agreeing wholeheartedly with his 'Fuck it! Fuck it all to hell and back!'

In fact, hearing him cursing the downfalling rain so loudly makes people start to smile, enjoying the wallow in self-pity that comes with bad weather.

'Aw, fuck it!' Mr Miller says again, shaking himself. 'There you are,' he says to me. An accusation: I am completely dry, ashamed to be so, having spent the last hour in here, before the rain. 'Will it never stop!' he announces to no one in particular, inserting his heavy frame in his usual place at the bar, waiting for a drink to be put in front of him. Always the same cheap French brandy, the same nod in acknowledgement when it's brought to him. 'It will never stop,' he says, half to me, shaking his head, a pendulous, sorrowful gesture. 'It'll just keep on and on and that will be it. Only more of the same old shit, without alteration or cease. Fuck it,' he growls, not unusually. Most things he says are black with venom or slippery with self-pity, impossible to reply to except in hopeless denial.

Heavy – that is perhaps the first word that would spring to mind if asked to describe Mr Miller, to pick him out from a crowd. 'He's the heavy one,' might sound odd, but to see him, you'd know what that meant. He's not fat, not at all, and he moves with a speed that is surprising in one so huge. But he has a broad back, shoulders, girth – large, stubborn proportions that he carries about with the force of a declaration, unavoidable in small spaces. About six five, he walks with his head tilted slightly, as though contemplating the sky, expecting new doom to fall upon him, and in this posture he only appears taller than he is, his shoulders thrust backwards. He is a man who always seems to be braced for, or guarding against something.

The strange thing is, he also seems happy. Not happy in the sense of being an obviously joyful sort. It is more something to do with being unfettered. A man without apparent burdens. He never seems to have any real problems, despite his complaints. Nothing ever appears to change him. This does not mean that he is implacable, far from it, but that he is adept at intransigence: he doesn't belong in the world, in the same way that other people might be said to belong in it.

His storming in here, bawling 'Fuck it!' is in fact nothing exceptional. This is his entire, often-expressed attitude to life. 'Powerless to change it,' is another of his familiar mutterings, usually to himself, under his breath. He is a great believer in his own impotence. His curses are in fact always deflations of some sort, his way of belittling any nuisance, like bad weather, by catching it in a curse. In this way, he avoids contact with all inconvenience, and appears to sail through life unruffled, aimlessly blasphemous, heaving that huge frame of his from home to here, here to home. It is rumoured that he is a writer, but no one has ever seen any evidence of a book.

Usually, he does precisely this: through the door, cursing, straight to the bar, French brandy before him – maybe five or six of those, which he drinks with methodical, considered sips, though without apparent relish – then out of the door into the night, listing slightly, head tilted skywards so that he seldom meets anyone's eyes, cursing still, though now more softly heard, since drowned out in the mess of raised voices around closing time. He seldom speaks directly to anyone, unless you count the mild rants cast sideways out of the corner of his mouth, to be picked up, or not, as the case may be, and he certainly doesn't seem to care either way.

But tonight, something is different. For a start, he's never addressed me directly before, if his 'There you are' can be said to count for that, which I suppose it can. He is almost smiling, too, something else he is seldom ever seen to do.

He stands there in front of his drink for a moment as the arrested conversations around him start up their slow modulation of fractured sound, made soft by the dense space and the constant thrum of rain outside, pounding the car rooftops and finger-drumming the glass of the window-panes. Then he takes a large brown paper parcel out from beneath his drenched coat. He hands it to the girl behind the bar, saying, 'Don't suppose you could put this on the radiator to dry it out, it's dreadfully wet.' Handing it over to her, he turns to me, as though assessing me closely for the first time, saying, 'That's that then.'

I have no idea, naturally, what he is talking about and from the weird, unfamiliar gleam in his eye, I'm not certain that I'm supposed to ask him either. So I just raise my glass slightly in acknowledgement and wait for him to go on, not sure that he will. He considers me slowly, not taking his eyes off me, so that I have to turn away. It makes me feel uncomfortable, his open, clear-sighted face like an indictment of my own muddy-headedness.

I think: happy? Why do people always describe him as happy? Erased would be a more accurate way of describing what I've just seen in his eyes, which is unsettling. As though he has got the whole place worked out, right down to every last one of us here, and has been considering the situation for some time, in secret, hiding behind his bland exterior and hugely unquestionable physical weight. He is not the kind of man who is open to challenges.

'I was listening to you the other day,' he says, quiet-spoken all of a sudden, unlike his usual ranting decibels. 'I was listening to you talking to someone, and whoever it was, I forget who, said, "Yes, yes, but someone who talks about killing themselves will never do it, of course." "No, of course not," you said, and then you both laughed like pretty little hyenas. I remember this clearly,' he says, still in an undertone. 'But, you see,' he goes on, 'that is simply not true.'

Then he finishes his drink and edges slightly away from me, almost as though that is it, the end of the matter and that's all he wanted to say. In fact, he is getting himself into a better position to give me a full rendition of his theory.

'You see, a person who talks about wanting to kill themselves is doing it for a reason, and the reason can sometimes be this: to make the idea real. Once it's real, then you can do what you want with it. Act upon it, or not, as the case may be. I know this, you see, because it is my particular area of study.'

'I thought you were a writer,' I say to him, trying not to meet his gaze.

'Of sorts,' he replies, 'more a philosopher. And you know that Platonic clap-trap about philosophers being people who spend their lives practising at being dead, well, there's a grain of truth in it, sure enough there is.'

He appears to consider this idea slowly for a few moments, turning it around in his mind as he takes another, longer swig from his glass of brandy, before starting up again in the same low tone of unusual deliberation.

'But it's harder than you might at first think,' he says, widening his eyes slightly as though for emphasis, 'practising at being dead. I know that what they meant by it was that communion-with-the-mind idea, putting you on a plane removed from the brute facts, in touch with Reality, and so forth. But if you think of it more in terms of a person trying to live their life *freed from desire*, then I think you're getting closer to the thing I mean: death as an ideal state. Unfettered by facts and the hungry, hopeful acquisition of facts. It's tricky. Almost impossible, and it's the *almost* that can catch you out. It has been my life's work, actually, the exposition and if you like expurgation of that *almost*, so that now I'm in precisely the position I've always wanted to get myself into, right from day one.'

Miller says this last thing with a chest-swell of pride, and I think: is he in fact insane? Because it's his pride which unnerves me the most: it is so full of conviction. I suspect this unease is stamped all across my face, because he smiles even more, nodding his head slightly, even tapping the side of his huge nose with a delicately extended finger, a bizarrely sleuth-like gesture, as much as to say, 'I know what's what, and your disbelieving face has just revealed to me that you, on the other hand, do not.'

'So how did I do it?' he asks me now, though apparently not expecting an answer, so I just shake my head and wait for him to go on. 'How, indeed. That would be to tell you everything. But anyway, the long and the short, to cut to the – and so forth, is that I'm ready. Now, I'm ready.'

He finishes his brandy, nods at the girl behind the bar for another and only now takes his eyes off me, tilting his head back once more into its familiar position. 'Do you want me to tell you how I came to this conclusion?' he asks the ceiling. 'It has taken me my whole life. From the beginning, though, that's the place to start. Am I right?'

He shoots me a fast, anxious look. I can tell that he's unused to telling people about himself, as though he isn't sure that he has the right. And it is his timidity that makes me curious to hear more: it seems to be so unlike him. So I smile at him in encouragement and he reflects my expression back at me, his face animated suddenly when before it had been blank with that strangely imperturbable paleness that I couldn't quite fathom. In fact, he is almost grinning when he takes a hefty swig of brandy before launching himself, like this:

'Now this is a very ordinary story,' he starts out, still smiling, though looking in earnest, too. 'I'm very young when it begins. I have hopes and I'm ambitious in a way that makes me feel constantly restless, my mother saying to me the whole time, "Itchy feet like yours will get you nowhere." A curse, is how it sounds to me, because my itchy feet are the only assets I have at this stage. So there I am. Young, restless. The usual thing. And with itchy feet, too. Soon enough, all my hopefulness gets me into trouble: I fall in love. This is at the age of thirteen, so I'm a precocious kid, didn't know any better. The girl, Veronica, was pretty as a pea. I can still see her now, precisely the way she looked, her face straight into my mind's eye, crash – like that,' (he cracks his forehead violently with his fist when he says this), 'straight there, at a moment's notice. This is true love we're talking about, even if I was a little fellow, not really wise to what it was all about. She was two years older than me, fifteen, and seemed to me to be an angel of some kind, perfectly placed to set me on my way in life.

'Then she dumped me. One day, came round to the house, she had the decency to do that, I suppose, and said, "I don't think things are working out between us. We shouldn't see each other again," that kind of line. Just words she'd picked up from the television, but said with the serious conviction of a little girl, plaits swinging along as ever when she left me, turning her slender back on me in the street.'

He pauses for a moment then, looking at himself in the mirror behind the bar. His eyes widen in surprise, as though he expected to see another person – his childhood self? – reflected there. His smile turns to a scowl and he makes a soft clucking noise at the back of his throat. His face darkens momentarily with disgust.

'Now, it is summertime. The end of summer. But a long, hot summer of the kind that withers trees and lawns, the whole thing almost ablaze with straw-dry lack of water. Dry as can be imagined. People too dry even to sweat. The rustle of dust in the streets making everyone nervous, as though there might be sudden fires. Spontaneous combustions to match my heart's fast blaze. My head was a perpetual threat of explosive dissatisfaction, and a crushing, humiliating sorrow for this little girl, Veronica, who had dumped me. Me! Just a child and I should have known better, but had trusted her with my hopes and the whole sorry show. Betrayed is how I felt. Though that doesn't do justice to the wildness of how I was feeling. Lost all sense of anything sane, hot brain in hotter head, heat outside, the whole thing dry and no chance of fecundity, that's how it felt. Infertile. Terminal. Without hope. Useless.'

As he says this, Miller raises his right hand to his forehead, touching the skin as though gauging its temperature. It looks doubtful that he will carry on, but he braces his shoulders, takes a couple more sips of brandy, his voice pitching lower as he continues.

'So I refused food, wouldn't get out of bed, didn't play, was miserable. I expect the adults all found this amusing as hell, seeing their sorrowing son acting like some kind of spurned romantic hero, withering away without recourse to sunlight and so on. Then, one day, it rained. Not any kind of rain. Rain like rivers running down from the sky. It looked like the end of the world! So much rain after so much drought, it caught everyone off-guard, more surprised than animals, without even their instincts to fall back on. Dumbstruck and shocked to their bones is how everyone was. Even the earth couldn't make sense of it, after so many weeks without water, this sudden drenching was impossible to absorb.'

He turns towards the window then, smiling at the sight of the streaming windows, darkening with rain and dusk. When he turns back to me, his eyes are shining.

'No one and nothing could take it in, is my point. We, everything, the whole scene, was in shock. No one more than me. But of course, I'm still not going out. So I watch the rain come down from behind glass, in my room, nose-pressing the window like a fugitive scared to take on the intrusions of ordinary life. That's when I make my decision.

Never again, I decide, would I let myself be as itchy-footed hopeful as I had been before, with the girl, falling in love so deadly complete as I had. The whole world, senseless, and who was I to change it? The end of pleasure, then, for me. Freed from desire.'

Miller's expression is still animated up until this point, his face jumping with the memory of his childhood sweetheart, visions of the way he was. Then it takes on the more familiar, inscrutable blankness, the shadow shutting down his features, stilling them as surely as if someone had blown the life out of them.

'So that's what I did,' he says, his lips barely moving, back once again to their muttering motion, opening only just enough to let the words out. 'You might think that that was the most idiotic thing a person could do,' he tells me. And I think: erased? Why can't I find the word for it? The most accurate description of how he looks is his own: freed from desire. It's as though his strongest impulse is merely the one to set his mouth in motion, telling me the things he's telling me, but without the need really to tell his story for any purpose other than itself, not hopeful for any effect. It is like an almost-corpse's last twitch, a verbal defecation, purely involuntary, as though the noose is already tightening around his neck and he is leaving the world without mental anguish, burdened by nothing beyond his body's efficient out-clearing of an insignificant story from his youth.

All he has left is memory, the sole residue of a life lived – as he says – freed from desire. Unstirred and silted up, the grains of recollection are almost dried out, too, and it's as though the rains hurtling earthwards outside have scattered themselves over the dusty seeds in his mind, revitalising his memory just enough for this involuntary-seeming exposition, though not enough to make anything grow there, just dry seeds of a desire that once was all-consuming, though now many years ago, another place and man entirely.

'And since then,' he goes on, 'there has never been a time when I have been able, truthfully, to stand in a room and say to someone: See that woman over there? She's my girlfriend, wife, whoever. There has never been a time like that. I have never been attached. I have had no desire for such a person. I decided I would not and I have never been caught out. That was it. I made the decision to be hopeful for nothing and I stuck by it, ever since that moment of realisation. Simply, that if a person has no hope, then they can be ready for anything, all disappointments, all triumphs, never caught out by life, not like the idiot earth, shocked into floods by the rain, too hopeful for water to be able to cope with the lovely excess of it when it eventually came down. I vowed I'd never be caught out in the same way – by love, for instance. And in this way, I've carried on. *I have carried on.*'

He repeats this last phrase under his breath. I think that I can detect an edge of incredulity in his voice. But maybe I'm mistaken. It is just the words themselves. Not even his belief in them. I wonder for a moment: could he be lying? But in his eyes, still the undermining of that hope of mine: nothing. Just eyeballs, glassy and unmysterious, without desire. And without that galvanising spike of need, what could a person amount to? There is no sense, nor hope of an impulse forwards without the shiver of desire to tremble their spirit into life.

'Aw, fuck it!' he says now, his mouth curving upwards into a smile without mirth. 'It just keeps on, more of the same old shit, without alteration or cease,' his glance tilts towards the window. I suppose he's referring to the rain.

'So,' he starts up again, head thrown backwards towards the ceiling, avoiding looking at me, though by this stage I am scrutinising his every move, wondering: could such a thing be possible? To have lived this way?

'The reason I tell you any of this stuff,' he says now, 'is for no reason other than a) because I had to tell someone and here you are, and b) because of what you were saying the other day, when I was eavesdropping.'

He chortles slightly when he says this, though perhaps he is just clearing his throat. 'I'm referring, of course, to your saying that a person who is going to kill themself never talks about it first, which I disagree with, you see, in every way possible. The reason being something of this kind: that when my darling Veronica dumped me, I decided to kill myself. But naturally, I was scared to do it. I told myself that the only reason for not doing it was that I couldn't quite shift my restless itchy-footedness – the one thing I had going for me. I had to be *doing something*, you see, whereas to kill myself I had to be ready and prepared to *do nothing* – be dead.

'So I decided to write down the reasons for and against killing myself. I started out with just a few ideas and then soon enough, bit by bit and overwhelmingly, the ideas got longer and longer and more and more involved, until, as the time tick-tocked by, it dawned on me that I was merely writing stories, different scenarios about all the circumstances that might bring a person, not always myself, to top themself – or not, which is the point: on the surface of it, most of those stories had nothing whatsoever to do with suicide. They were all to do with love and the pursuit of it. Love as the greatest goal of all humankind, the big picture that everyday events had to try to measure up to, seldom did.

'By this stage, I'm getting older. By every stage! The dull

incrementation of time and delay, practising, preparing myself in various ways, for being dead. That's what I told myself at the start. And in the end, that's the sum of what I've done. That's all there is to it. Ah! The rain!' he finishes, downing another brandy, his eye-rolling gaze taking in the pelting sky, a disinterested-seeming sweep across the whole scene – bar, sky, the street outside.

He turns now to the girl behind the bar. 'Is that parcel dry yet?' he asks her.

'I'll just check, Mr Miller, won't be a second.' She disappears out the back to check on his once-dripping brown paper package.

She comes back in. 'It needs a bit more time,' she tells him, 'not long, though.'

'Fuck it all,' he says, in an amiable fashion, not angry in any way. Impassive. 'I have to go. I'll end up being late. It can wait. I can't. So it'll have to stay here. It doesn't matter.'

He's smiling again now. And this time something that looks like genuine happiness or amusement edges its way across his face as he turns to me. 'I do appreciate you being so patient, listening to me go on like that. It's really very good of you to listen.'

'Not at all. I've enjoyed it,' I tell him truthfully. 'Let's do it again,' I say to him, not expecting his reply.

'No, we will never do it again,' he says with no trace of regret, wistfulness or melodrama. Just dead-pan honest. I suspect he's making some smart-arse Heraclitian, never-jump-into-the-same-river-twice kind of remark, so I just smile back at him, unperturbed.

He nods in farewell, slightly, starting to turn to leave the bar, then remembering. 'When the parcel is dried out, would you mind keeping it safe for me?' he asks, blushing: he knows that he has been caught out. Certainly, he is not freed from the desire that I should keep that parcel safe for him. I pretend not to notice. His face glazes over once more into inexpression.

'Sure,' I tell him, 'sure, I'll do that.'

He turns then, leaves the bar, and I start my familiar, well-trodden sink towards insensibility, softly into the grave of the night with the lovely rain limpid-hurling outside, me safe behind glass and dry, content, too, in a way, comforted by the sound of his final, 'Fuck it all!' as he goes out into the rain.

Around closing time, still with no sign of the rain letting up, I ask for the parcel, now dry as dust, crinkled at the edges, so that the paper has partly come away from the top and I can see that it is a manuscript of some kind. Curious, bleary with booze, I take a peek at the title page, which, in large type, reads: 'LEARNING HOW TO DIE, A LIFE, or, AFTER VERONICA.'

I laugh quietly to myself as I rewrap the manuscript in paper and stuff it into a plastic bag against the rain. I stand for a moment at the door, contemplating how godawfully wet I'm going to get before I make it home. Even here, a few feet inside the doorway, slanting drops have started to drench me. I put Miller's manuscript inside my coat and wrap myself up more tightly against the cold which is bitter now that the long nights, ever darker, are starting to carry with them the scent of dead summer, winter absolutely on its way, and soon.

As I start to leave, the bar still heaving with late drinkers, a man rushes in, one of the regulars, pale with shock, stumbling over his words as he tells the news to the owner, DG, addressing him as though he were ruler of this little kingdom of drinkers and as such had to be the first to know. Out of breath, holding his forehead in surprise, wet through and high-shouldered, the man cuts across the murmur of inebrious sound to say, 'Mr Miller! He's dead! They're just taking him down now. He hanged himself in an alley off the square, from a lamp-post.'

I stand there in the doorway, turned from the scene, watching the rainy night outside, listening half-ways through the sides of my hearing to the messenger's description of how they found him, just now, this very minute, police there already, all the people pointing and so on. I think someone says, 'But he was just in here, only a few moments ago,' indignantly. I thought it sounded like indignation in his voice. I want to correct him, too, because it was over an hour ago that he left, at least an hour. And I wonder what he did in the intervening time?

Did he have any moments of doubt? Did he walk about in the rain? He must have been drenched through to the skin with it, in that case. Did he speak to anyone else, after he spoke to me, or was his parting shot to the world his 'Fuck it all!' as he went out of here into the night? Was I the last person he spoke to? That thought horrifies me, though not as much as the thought of his smiling eyes, just for those moments of talking about his childhood sweetheart, his attempts to drown fond memories of her in the insane downpourings of his intransigent convictions, scratched across all his desire, for a lifetime.

I leave the bar, head out into the rain, the night. The same old shit, without alteration or cease. Fuck it all. He was right about that much. Always the same old shit.

Better than Well

DAREN KING

When he awoke, the room was beautiful. He had never seen the room before. It was more than just walls and ceiling and floor: the objects and furniture were a part of the room. He himself was a part of the room. He was on the bed on his back. He lay beneath the blankets and looked up at the ceiling. The ceiling was painted white, but light shone in through the curtain and gave the ceiling colour. The walls, also, were coloured by the light. They were uneven and pitted. They had been papered and the paper had been painted bright white. The paint covered both the wallpaper and the many nails and picture hooks that had not been removed. Although the walls were uneven and pitted they did not look bad: they looked good.

It was a beautiful room. It was coloured by light that came into the room from outside, in through the curtains. The curtains were thin and did not prevent the light from coming in. The light became coloured as it came through, filling the room and everything inside it with colour. It was the colour that made the room beautiful. He had seen the room many times but it had not been beautiful.

He got out of bed and crossed the room and lifted the curtain. It was morning: the source of light was the morning sun. He stood by the window and held the curtain open and looked around the room. There was something about the room that he liked. He liked everything about the room: it was beautiful. The sunlight was bright and made everything look bright. Everything in the room was bright and had its own colour. Each colour was distinct and filled the shape of the thing to which it belonged.

He turned back to the window. The sunlight shone so bright that it made him close his eyes. With eyes closed he could still see the light, but in red. He opened his eyes, fully opened the curtain and stepped away from the window.

As he moved about inside the room, the room changed. He was a part of the room and could change it by moving about inside it. It was not just that the room looked different when looked at from a different position: the room did actually change. When you moved you changed and when you changed you changed not only yourself but also anything that you were a part of. Moving yourself was like moving the furniture or the things that were on the furniture. To move a thing would be to change the thing. There was nothing that he could not change, that could not be changed. He sat on the chair and thought about change.

Leaning forward, he picked up a photograph from the desk. He looked at the face in the photograph and smiled. This was how a baby felt when it recognised a face. He looked at the face and smiled. The face smiled, too. It had been smiling before he smiled and would continue to smile if he stopped. The person had been smiling at the time that the photograph had been taken and the smile had gone into the photograph. The smile in the photograph was not a real smile but a photograph of a smile. The camera had not taken the smile but had taken a photograph of the smile. He understood that the photograph was just a photograph but that the smile on the face of the person had been real and would have been felt inside.

He placed the photograph on the front of the desk and looked at it. Although he had not taken the photograph himself, he did own it. He could look at it and smile or look at it and not smile. He did not even have to look at it: he was free. Standing from the chair, he looked around the room and smiled.

As he smiled he found that his smile was real. It was not a photograph of a smile but a real smile, a smile that came from inside and moved outside. It moved out from his inside and onto his face and out into the room. The smile was real and the room, too, was real. Nothing had been real and now it was real. It was all real.

The odd thing about the room was that the more real it became the more like a photograph it became. The room was like a photograph that he himself was a part of. It was vivid like a photograph and, like a photograph, could be looked at. There was nothing in front of it, blocking it. Nothing stood between his sight and the room. He did not need to analyse the room to see it: to see the room all he had to do was look.

As he straightened the blankets over the bed he thought about how everything was its own opposite, how everything that was good was bad and everything that was bad was also good. He did not like this thought and did not want to think it.

The moment the bed was made, he straightened his back

and the thought was gone. This was good: it had been a bad thought. If a thought was bad you did not have to think it. Thoughts were not things that flew at you when you were making the bed, but things that you made, like the bed, and you need only make the things that you wanted to make. You would think only the things that you wanted to think. Bad thoughts could not hurt you: you could not become mad by thinking the wrong thought.

He wondered what it would be like to be mad, to have thoughts that continued without end. He was glad that he was not like that, that he was not mad.

Although he was not mad, when he closed his eyes he saw colours. He closed his eyes and wondered why it was no longer dark. He had always been afraid of the dark but he was not afraid of it now because it had gone.

Perhaps darkness meant that you were normal and colours meant that you were mad. But then, as long as he had the colours it did not matter. He wanted only to smile and cover his eyes and see the colours.

It did not matter. Nothing mattered, and that was a good thing. It was enough to just lie there on the bed. He had something inside him that made nothing matter. He lay there on the bed and thought about how it did not matter.

He thought of a word: fluoxetine. The word had been on the packet. He took the packet from the desk and read the word. He wanted to remove the word and hang it on the wall. It would hang on a wall in the street and nobody would be able to pass it without seeing it and reading it and wanting to know what it meant. He read the word and the words and figures that were printed on either side of it: 30 fluoxetine caps 20mg. Take one daily. Mr Daren King. 04/02/00. Beneath these words was a picture: happiness. The happiness was not real happiness but was a picture depicting happiness, symbolised by a sun. The sun symbolised the happiness that the capsules put inside him when he put the capsules inside him.

The important thing about the capsules was that they were his. The capsules were his and the pillow was his. He was free and he could move things and he could hold the pillow over his eyes. Lying on the bed, he lifted the pillow and held it over his eyes. Although the pillow prevented the sunlight from shining onto his face, his face felt sunny. It was something inside him. It was something he had taken.

He hated the thing that he had taken. He did not give a fuck about it. It was because he loved it that he did not give a fuck about it. If you could love something and not give a fuck about it then you could be free.

Skunk

GEOFF DYER

In April 1999 I spent several days in Paris researching a 'walk' for the *Time Out Book of Paris Walks*. My walk was in the eleventh arrondissement where I had lived, off and on, for much of the early nineties, but I was actually staying with my friends Hervé and Mimi in the eighth, on rue de l'Elysée, opposite the presidential palace. For dinner on the evening of my arrival, Hervé said, he had invited a new friend of theirs, a beautiful young woman called Marie Roget.

When Marie arrived she was, if not beautiful in the way Mimi is, extremely attractive. She was tall (almost six foot) with calm green eyes and what, from my cheaply barbered point of view, seemed expensively styled black hair. Although dressed like a gas pump attendant on a space station – her trousers, manufactured from some ultra-synthetic heat- and cold-resistant fabric, consisted entirely of pockets – she had a Parisian fondness for debate and strident argument. When during the course of dinner I declared myself 'totally pro-Nato, a 100 per cent in favour of bombing Serbia', she found it incredible that 'a so-called intellectual could say – let alone think – something so stupid'.

'Who said I was an intellectual?' I said.

'Hervé,' she said.

'Ah, he must have been teasing,' I said.

I liked her even though she smoked a great deal, more than Hervé and Mimi who are fairly heavy smokers. After dinner, drunk, I dropped a wine glass. As we cleared up the curves and splinters of glass Marie cut her finger and a few drops of blood landed on my battered trainers. She ran her hand under the cold tap in the bathroom and I wrapped a Band-Aid around her long slim finger – an action which alluded, however medically, to the possibility of marriage. The atmosphere between us changed, softened, and we arranged to meet the following day so that we could research my walk together. She wrote her number on the last page of my notebook, leaving a faint smear of blood as she did so. Her handwriting was bold, unambiguous.

'Call me after lunch,' she said as we kissed goodbye.

Hervé was leaving Paris the following afternoon to visit a friend in Marseille. We met for lunch on his way to the Gare de Lyon, in a restaurant in the eleventh where I had spent the morning researching my walk. Hervé insisted – as he did about all the women he introduced me to – that Marie was dying to go to bed with me. I insisted – as I always do – that he was wrong, that, in any case, of all the women he had introduced me to, there was only one I wanted to go to bed with and that was Mimi. After we had said goodbye I called Marie and we arranged to meet at the Café Charbon on Oberkampf.

She turned up exactly on time, wearing baggy combats and a pale T-shirt with something Japanese written on the front. So, she said after we had had a coffee (my fourth of the day), what did I want to do? I said that it would be very useful for my walk if we could get stoned. Marie was happy to try, even though grass never had any effect on her.

We spent a long time trying to find a place where we could get discreetly high. In one little park there were too many mothers and young children who might have thought we were junkies; in another, too many young kids whom we thought were junkies. There were windows, eyes, everywhere. Eventually we found a bench by the Canal St Martin. Evidently this was quite a spot for stoners; on the next bench along a couple were already smoking a joint. As I filled a pipe Marie said again that she had tried several times to smoke grass but it never had any effect on her.

'Oh well, let's hope this does,' I said. Although we had only met the night before I felt perfectly relaxed with her, possibly because I had no sexual feelings towards her. This was partly because she smoked cigarettes, partly because I had a girlfriend in England (though I did not mention this, of course). I don't know if she had any kind of sexual feelings for me. Probably not – I had learned long ago to set no store by anything Hervé said in this regard – but I think she *was* curious because I did not fit any of the moulds from which Parisian men were cast. This was the first afternoon she had spent with a forty-year-old intellectual who had nothing intelligent to say about – and little interest in – anything except night-clubs and smoking dope. I lit the pipe, took a couple of hits and passed it to her. It was obvious that, although she smoked cigarettes continually, she had no idea how to do this.

'Hold it in,' I said, coughing. 'For as long as you can.' She tried again, passed the pipe back to me, and breathed out. I took another big hit and passed the pipe to her again. A barge was going through a lock on the canal. The effort of negotiating these locks seemed so enormous as to take all the fun out of travelling by canal. I was glad that I was sitting here watching, getting stoned, rather than becoming actively involved in the interminable chore of lock negotiation, but I would have preferred not even to have seen it. I was surprised how quickly I was high.

'Are you feeling anything yet?' I said.

'No. Are you?'

'I'm completely blasted,' I said.

'What is it like?'

'It's difficult to say. Like being stoned. It's not like anything else.'

We walked a little further, unsure of where we were going because of the profound – some would say disturbing – spatial disorientation that is a characteristic of skunk. I was noticing everything but as soon as I noticed one thing I noticed something else and so, in a way, I was oblivious to everything. We were no longer by the canal, we were walking along a street, jammed with cars, parked and moving, though even the moving cars were stationary. The dull sky had brightened slightly. Marie waited outside while I went into a shop – our mouths were terribly dry – and bought a couple of bottles of Evian.

'Feeling anything?' I asked. The water was so cold it made my teeth hurt.

'I feel funny.'

'How?'

'I don't think I like it.'

'D'you feel ill?'

'No, but I –'

'– Don't worry about it. Just enjoy it.'

'What was that stuff you gave me?'

'Grass.'

'No. It can't have been.'

'It was. Skunk. Very strong grass. But you only had a little, so don't worry.' I took her by the arm, smiled, and we walked along like a nice Parisian couple out for a stroll. If we could get through the next few minutes I was confident we would have a good time. We had not been strolling for long, though, when Marie said she wanted to sit down. There was a café over the road so we crossed, carefully, and sat down at an outside table.

'Where are we?' she said.

'I don't know. Rue something . . .' I looked around but could not see a sign.

'Where are we?' she said again.

'Paris. In a café. Quite a nice café,' I said. 'A Parisian café, if you will.' Walking had meant that Marie was not able to focus entirely on how weird she was feeling. Now that we were seated, however, there was nothing to distract her.

'Would you like something to drink?' I said.

'What was that stuff you gave me?'

'Grass. Just grass,' I said, though whether this was strictly true is a moot point. Many people regard skunk as a genetically modified product and boycott it accordingly.

Marie shook her head. 'Why did you do this?'

'Do what?'

'Give me that stuff.'

'I thought it would be fun. And useful for my work.'

'Why?'

'It enables one to enter the dream-space of the city,' I said.

'Why do you want to do that?'

'It's a version of the city I like.'

'I don't want to be in your city. I want to be in my city. Where is my city? Why can't we be in my city?'

The waiter came over. I ordered two coffees even though, as well as being bombed on skunk, I was already feeling wired from too much coffee.

When the waiter had gone Marie, looking pale, asked, 'Why me?'

'What do you mean?'

'Of all the people in Paris, why me? Why me?'

'Because I met you yesterday and I thought you were cool. I thought we could hang out, research my walk. I thought it would be fun.'

She shook her head which was, in a way, fair comment. It was obvious that she was not having fun. Far from it. She did not know where she was. Who she was. Even *if* she was. Skunk is like that, especially for the first twenty minutes or so which can be like pandemonium. That's why people who like it – people like me – like it.

'What have you done to me?'

'Listen, it's only grass. However strange you're feeling it can't have any bad effect on you physically. If I had given you a pill, let's say, and you began feeling funny, then I would be worried because maybe it could have some physical consequences. But this is only grass. It's physically harmless. It's just in your head. If you relax and go with it, it will be fine. It will be nice.'

She shook her head. The waiter came back with the coffees neither of us wanted. He glanced at Marie and saw, I think, that all was not quite well. I was totally out of it too but intent on behaving properly, on saying and doing all the right things, on trying to reassure her.

After a while she said, 'You're not really with *Time Out*, are you?'

'Of course I am.'

'Who sent you?' she said, abruptly, and with such vehemence that it sounded like a line from a thriller.

'That is a line you utter,' I said, 'while grabbing someone by the lapels and shoving them up against the wall of a garbage-strewn alley. It's a line to be hissed, your face inches from the person you're hissing at. "Who sent you? Who sent you?"' This little speech made no impression on her and so, smirking slightly, I added, '*Time Out* sent me.'

My notebook was on the table. She picked it up and began looking through the scrawled notes I had made for my contribution to the *Time Out Book of Paris Walks*. My handwriting is impossible for anyone else to read – I have trouble reading it myself sometimes – but she was staring intently at every page.

'You're not writing a guide at all,' she said, a look of vacant realisation in her green eyes.

'Of course I am.'

'You're putting me in a novel, aren't you?' she said, each new page confirming her suspicions. Still smirking, I shook my head. She shook hers too and turned to the last page of the book, the page with people's phone numbers.

'Why do you have all these numbers?'

'They're people I know in Paris, people I hoped to have time to see.'

'Why is my number here?'

'You wrote it in there yesterday,' I said, relieved that she appeared not to have noticed the dried smudge of blood. She took a biro from her bag – the same biro she had used the day before – and began trying to cross out her name and number. Unfortunately the pen had run out of ink since then and so she began using it as a chisel, gashing out parts of that page and the three or four underneath. It was a gesture of self-obliteration, almost of suicide. The sight of all those telephone numbers had put another idea in her head as well.

'I need to make a call,' she said. For some time now I had realised that she was not the adventurous free spirit she had seemed the day before. But when she said this, when she said she wanted to make a call, I saw that she was someone who often spent evenings hanging out on the phone, chatting to friends, many of whom had boyfriends and did not live nearby. I could feel the loneliness, the skunk loneliness that was now overwhelming her. At the same time, she had seen something in me.

'You are evil,' she said. Skunk is like that: it takes the normal dope-smoker's paranoia and raises it to a level of reeling expressionist insight. This is not without its plus points. You feel the paranoia so palpably, even in situations in which there is no threat or danger, that skunk offers a chance to experience it in uniquely pure, uncut form – as dread, almost – with no anchoring in external events. Or at least that is what I used to think. I have since stopped smoking skunk because it was making me too paranoid.

'Please listen,' I said. 'Trust me. I know that's what you feel you can't do but you must trust me. I promise that nothing bad will happen to you.' I reached for her hand and she did not snatch it away. I held it the way you hold the hand of an injured or dying person, not as you take the hand of a young woman in a Paris café you are on the brink of making a pass at. While I was speaking she seemed to be listening but as soon as I stopped she was off again.

'I have to make a call,' she said. This was not a good idea for several reasons. To get to the phone she would have to walk into the bar, possibly ask the barman where the phone was. Any friend she called would be alarmed at the way she sounded, the way she didn't know where she was, the way she was with this sinister English intellectual she barely knew. The friend would ask to speak to the barman and before we knew it we would be in trouble – and keeping us both out of trouble was my main concern.

'How about this?' I said. 'You sit here and I'll phone Mimi. She knows us both. She will reassure you.' Marie shook her head. Determined to have her way and make a call, she stood up. I was torn between physically restraining her – thereby making her more frightened, possibly creating a commotion – and . . .

It was too late anyway. She was walking into the bar. I watched her disappear into the back of the café, relieved that she did not have any communication with the barman. Now that she was gone I was aware of how hard I had been concentrating on acting normally, reasonably. I was feeling the effort of trying to remain calm as a physical sensation, of extreme tension, in my head. I wanted to behave correctly – to do the right thing, as they say – but another part of me was becoming a little irritated that my afternoon's research was being so thoroughly fucked up.

After a few minutes Marie came back. As she did, for the first time that day, the sun came out. She had not made a call because she could not remember anyone's number. Good, I thought. Thank heavens for small blessings. And since sitting down had not made her feel any better, it seemed a good idea if we resumed our abortive stroll. I left forty francs on the table for our untouched coffees and we got up. Unfortunately, walking presented her with new problems. Out of the corner of her eye she kept seeing things – a black dog whose tail had been chopped off, a butcher's shop full of pink meat, a torso of kebab in a Greek restaurant – things she didn't like, things that made her frightened. One of these things was me. Which is why, presumably, she announced that she wanted to take a taxi. This threw into even sharper relief the same dilemma that had confronted me when she had wanted to make a phone call. She may have been freaking out but, while she was under my custodianship, even though she was having a terrible time, nothing could happen to her. However bad she was feeling she was better off under my protection. While I was thinking this she hailed a taxi. The taxi pulled over. She opened the door and began getting in. I could have pulled her out of the taxi, I could have got in the taxi myself, but she was in the taxi and I was standing on the pavement and I had done neither. I bent down and glanced at the driver. She pulled the door to and they drove off. One moment the taxi was there, at the kerb, and the next moment there was just the kerb and the oil-stained road and the shops opposite.

For a few moments I was relieved that she was gone. Then I became worried that she would not remember where she lived. No sooner had I thought this than I became convinced that the driver was going to abduct, rape or kill her. I could imagine the scene in the car as vividly as if I were there, as if mine were the eyes she saw in the driver's mirror, glancing at her as she sat rigid, white, clutching her bag, heading through the city which no longer had any direction or familiarity. It seemed certain that in the course of the next couple of days her body – her partly clothed body, as they say – would be discovered in the Bois de Boulogne. Stupidly, I had neglected to check the number plate . . .

I walked for a few minutes and then stopped at a café where the floor had just been cleaned. A smell of ammonia filled the place. I ordered my fifth coffee of the day and went to the toilet where I avoided making eye contact with the mirror. My penis, as happens when I am nervous or stoned or have drunk too much coffee (all three on this occasion), had shrunk dramatically: it was nothing but wrinkled foreskin and I found it difficult to piss. Then, when I had finished pissing, I found it difficult to stop completely. I should have got in the taxi with her. I kept replaying that moment, the moment when it was possible to have acted differently, but the outcome was always the same.

When I returned to my table I made a few notes, of things she had said, in case, one day, I wanted to use what had happened in a novel or story. I had a sharp sense of her in the taxi, of the driver's eyes and the neon dread of the city as it sped past. By now they had been driving for quite a time but her apartment was not getting any nearer. She couldn't tell which quartier she was in. Everywhere looked like everywhere else and nowhere looked like anywhere. I turned to the back of the notebook where she had erased her name and number. Seeing the brown smear of blood I remembered the drops that had fallen onto my trainers. I looked down at them but they were so grubby that the incriminating blood would only be forensically apparent. I deliberately asked the waiter, in English, where we were, what time it was. I got him to point out where we were in my *Plan de Paris*. I made sure that he would remember me. My mouth was drier than ever.

Before leaving, I called Mimi and explained what had happened. She said she would phone Marie at her apartment. Unsure what else to do I continued researching my walk. I walked down Popincourt (the street where I used to live) and Basfroi to rue de Charonne which, oddly, was quite deserted. The building on the corner there had not been renovated since the time of Atget and looked, consequently, as if it had been squatted by ghosts. Remembering what Benjamin had said of Atget – that he photographed Paris as if it were the scene of a crime – I walked down Keller back to rue de la Roquette. Twilight was falling. People were hurrying and strolling, heading home or going out or just lingering. All the bars and café terraces were full of Parisians smoking and drinking, and the street was crowded too. Glad to be among people again, I mingled with the crowd, looking in shop windows, heading in the direction of the Bastille.

At nine o'clock I met a friend for dinner at Chez Paul and then took the Métro back to the eighth. As I entered rue de l'Elysée a gendarme asked where I was going. This always happens, because of the proximity of the presidential palace. Remaining calm, I explained that I was staying with friends who lived at number 20 and he waved me on.

Mimi answered the door wearing a white bath robe. She had just washed her hair and wrapped it in a thick towel turban. I had hoped that by now Marie would have called, saying that she was at home and feeling better, but there had been no response to the message left by Mimi. I suggested calling again but Mimi said not to worry, Marie would probably call in the morning, a little embarrassed, but perfectly OK.

'Yes,' I said, but it seemed just as likely that, if we did get a call, it would be the police saying everything was far from OK.

Mimi had just opened a bottle of wine. In the fridge, she said. I filled a glass for myself, topped up Mimi's and told her in more detail about what had happened. I emphasised the funny side and drew attention to how correctly I had behaved. Basically, I made light of the whole episode. Mimi sat on the sofa. Her toenails were painted a lovely pale green. I took my shoes off – what with one thing and another I had been on the trudge practically all day – and stretched out on the seat opposite with my feet on the coffee table. From this low angle I could see a crescent moon, hanging above the presidential palace as though an Islamic republic had just been proclaimed. This impression was enhanced when Mimi got up and played a record of an old man singing in Arabic – it was a goatherd's lament, I think. She dried her hair vigorously and then hung the towel in the bathroom and sat on the sofa again, her legs curled under her. Her hair was still damp. I poured more wine. I had just glanced at the clock – it was almost twelve thirty – when the phone rang.

Not as Bad as This

MATT THORNE

Waterloo station. I arrived early, but Chloë was already waiting. She'd dressed exactly as instructed, long black dress, the blue overcoat I'd bought her in '92, forties-style shoes and her dark brown hair up at the back. She was standing on the tips of her toes and when I kissed her I gently placed my palm on her hip.

'Our train's in five minutes. Need anything?'

I shook my head, disturbed by the discoloration around her light blue eyes and wondering why I'd told her not to wear make-up. 'Did you stay up with him last night?'

She nodded. 'He's so excited about you coming back.'

'Lucky him.'

'How did your girlfriend react?'

'Smashed stuff up.'

She looked at me. I could tell she was trying to decide if I was telling the truth. I smiled back and she carried on looking nervous, tapping my arm as the number of our platform came up.

The train was half-full. We'd avoided rush hour, but the majority of passengers were still people returning home after work. Chloë kept nodding off, killing the conversation. We got out at Surbiton and started walking towards the bus stop.

'Let's get a taxi.'

'I can't afford it,' Chloë complained.

'I'll pay.' We started walking. 'Although I don't have any money on me.'

She sighed and took out her purse. 'I think I can just about afford it. You can pay me back tomorrow.'

We joined the back of the taxi queue. The cabs came quickly and we were soon on our way to Chloë's. She looked back from the window and said in a gentle tone, 'There is something you need to know.'

'OK.'

'My dad hasn't spoken at home for the last three months. At first we thought he was the same at work, but it seems he's fine there.'

'Hasn't spoken? You mean, nothing at all?'

'Um, he grunts and groans and cries, but no proper words. You remember the second time I was in hospital? Well, that's what he's like now.'

'God.'

'He may be different with you. My mum thinks when he sees you he'll start talking again.'

'So when you said before that he's happy about me coming back, how could you tell?'

'He started giggling.'

*

Chloë paid the taxi driver and we went into the house. There was a note from Chloë's mother on the table, telling us there was food in the kitchen. I took my purple and black sportsbag up to the bedroom. My old video was still on top of Chloë's television. Sixteen pounds in a second-hand shop seven years ago and still going strong. I walked across and pressed eject, curious about what she'd been watching. *Smooth Talk*. I walked back out to the landing and shouted downstairs, 'Where am I going to sleep?'

'It's up to you,' Chloë shouted back, 'I've put the camp-bed in Dad's study, but you can move it into my room.'

I went down into the kitchen. 'I'm not sure I like either of those options.'

Chloë looked pained. 'I can't have you in my bed, Rob, it'll kill my back.'

'I don't want to be in your bed. I want to be in the lounge.'

She looked at me. 'Are you sure? You'll have to fold it up every morning.'

'That's OK. What are we having to eat?'

She picked up a slice of meat and fed it to me. 'Wolf food.'

Chloë's sister returned home just as we were finishing dinner. She had her girlfriend Erica with her. The two of them had been a couple since before I got together with Chloë. Both girls looked very similar. They had identical short brown bobs and today were both wearing padded jackets, Diesel jeans and Buffalos. Erica wore a blue Knicks baseball T-shirt, Jane a plain black vest.

'There's food in the kitchen,' Chloë told her sister.

Jane stared at me. I smiled back, wondering whether she'd been told about me coming here, but her face was impossible to read.

*

It was almost ten when Chloë's mum came home. She looked less unsure than I remembered, maybe because she'd dyed her hair black. We were all playing Articulate around the dining-table, Jane being a boardgame fanatic. I got up from the table and walked across. Chloë's mum kissed me on the lips.

'Mum,' Chloë said loudly, shocked.

'What? I'm pleased to see him.'

Later, I asked Chloë's mum what time Tony might return, and where she thought he might be. She rubbed her eyes. 'Sometimes he doesn't get back until two. I don't know where he goes. Are you going to wait up?'

Chloë looked over. 'Rob wants to sleep in the lounge.'

'Don't you want to sleep with Chloë?'

'Mum,' she said, 'my back.'

'Oh, right. What about the study?'

'No,' I said, 'I don't like being surrounded by books.'

'OK, but Tony might wake you. He tends to spend most nights in the back garden. And I wouldn't go to sleep before he gets back. Just in case he gets scared when he sees you.'

'But he knows I'm here?' I asked, nervous.

'Oh yeah. I mean, he knew this morning.'

Chloë's mother went to bed first. Erica and Jane wanted to see an old episode of *Grace Under Fire* on the Paramount Channel, so the four of us sat watching that. When it reached the first ad break, Chloë got up to go to bed.

'I'll come with you,' I whispered.

'Why?'

'I want to watch you undress.'

Jane overheard. 'Do you want to see Chloë naked?'

'I was only joking,' I said quickly, feeling embarrassed.

Jane ignored my protests and took my hand. 'Come upstairs.'

I looked back at Chloë and Erica. Neither of them seemed especially annoyed, so I allowed myself to be led out of the lounge and up the stairs. When we reached Chloë's mum's room, Jane opened the door and turned on the light. Chloë's mum twisted on the queen-size bed, pulling the duvet down and squinting at us.

'What's wrong?'

'Nothing,' said Jane. 'I just wanted to show Rob Erica's painting.'

'Oh,' she replied, turning to look up at the three foot by six canvas hung above the bed. It was a lifesize portrait of Chloë, naked and standing by the mirrored wardrobe in her bedroom. It didn't surprise me to discover that Chloë's parents had a full-frontal of their daughter above their bed, but I did momentarily wonder whether this had contributed to her dad's derangement. I also wondered if Jane had been jealous of her girlfriend while she was painting Chloë.

'It's a beautiful picture,' I told her.

'I'm not sure she got Chloë's cunt quite right,' her mother noted. 'It's more impressionistic than the rest of her body.'

Jane smiled. 'I think Erica chickened out there. But it does make the whole painting easier on the eye.'

'She's an excellent artist,' Chloë's mum concluded, 'but if Rob wants a proper look he'll have to wait until the morning. Goodnight, you two.'

She burrowed back down in the bedclothes. Chloë was waiting for me on the landing. Her cheeks were red. Jane left us alone, returning to her girlfriend downstairs.

'You can watch me if you want to,' she said, looking at the floor. 'I was aware that would be part of the agreement. And if you want to do other stuff too, that's OK. I want to make up for things being difficult with your girlfriend.'

I put my fingers beneath her chin and gently lifted her

head. She continued avoiding my eye.

'Look at me.' She did so. 'Things aren't just difficult. I've sacrificed my relationship to come here.'

'I know,' she said, 'and I'm ready to do anything in return.'

I smiled. 'That's a generous offer. Shall we go into your bedroom?'

She nodded and opened the door. It occurred to me as I sat on the bed that I didn't yet know whether I would make a good sadist. I also couldn't tell if Chloë would draw pleasure from our arrangement. I thought of the painting I had just seen and wondered what it said about Chloë that she was prepared to pose naked for her sister's lesbian lover. Had she known where the painting would end up, and was that sacrifice similar to the one she was making now? It did somehow make perfect sense for her image to be hanging there. Everyone wanted to see Chloë naked. Not in the same way that people wanted to see a supermodel naked, but because it was the only way for her to prove her virtue. She was an English *Gold Heart* girl, destined to end up alone in the woods. And this was the real reason our relationship hadn't worked, as I'd only been interested in making her happy.

She stood by her mirrored wardrobe. 'Shall I just get undressed normally?'

'Don't do anything yet. Just let your hair down.'

She did so. 'Can I sit?'

'No, not yet. Do you still keep a diary?'

She shook her head. 'Not since you read it.'

'Any other writings? Stories? Poems?'

'No.'

'What about your old diaries?'

'I burnt them.'

'Why?'

'I didn't want to remember the way I used to be. And because of what you said, when you were angry.'

'What did I say?'

'That I perverted things. And didn't remember them right.'

Chloë was clearly near tears, and I wondered whether it was my questions or her memories that were upsetting her. But I felt certain she wanted me to be stern. So I asked, 'How many men have you been with since we broke up?'

'Two.'

'Who?'

'You don't know them.'

I looked away and sighed heavily, wanting her to think I was exasperated by her. 'Kneel down with your back to me.'

She did so.

'Now lift up your hair.'

'Like this?'

I realised she was trembling. 'You're not scared, are you, Chloë'?'

'Yes,' she said, 'but it's not just you. It's my lack of sleep, and the emotion. I'm all worked up.'

'OK,' I said, that's enough for tonight. Get some sleep.'

'Will you be able to cope when Dad comes home?'

'Yes. I'll say hello and go to bed.'

Jane and Erica soon went upstairs, leaving me alone in the lounge. I flicked through the cable stations until I found The Box and left it on quietly in the background as I unravelled the sleeping bag and duvet. I love the run of videos on that channel, the erratic selection somehow giving a perfect insight into the minds of people up watching and calling in their selections that late at night.

*Metallica, Christina Aquilerra, Insane Clown Posse, Slipknot, Ol'
Dirty Bastard* and so on, an endless party with a play-list
selected by insomniac crazies.

I wondered if Tony watched television when he stayed
up all night, and if he was ever tempted to call in to *The
Box*. What would he ask for? Santana, probably, or Van
Morrison. The video clock told me it was coming up to two.

Time to wake Chloë.

I didn't bother knocking on her bedroom door, but went
straight in and shook her awake.

'Urh,' she said, 'Rob?'

She looked terrible, which was probably unsurprising
seeing as I'd just interrupted her first few hours sleep in two
days.

'I've just realised I've forgotten my contact-lens stuff.'

'Can't you put them in water for the moment?'

'No.'

'You used to put them in water. I can get you some
solution in the morning.'

'No, these are new lenses. Putting them in water will
make them deteriorate and could be really dangerous for
my eyes.'

She turned on her side. 'Is Dad home?'

'Not yet.'

'There aren't any all-night chemists round here.'

'I thought we could get a cab.'

'So you need money? Is that why you woke me up?'

'No I was hoping you would come with me. I don't feel
safe going on my own.'

'Are you sure you need me to come with you? I'm so
tired, Rob.'

'Please, Chloë.'

Her eyes were open now, and her bare feet swung down from the bed to plant themselves on the carpet. She was wearing a plain white old-fashioned nightgown and her hair was sexily messed up. She stood up and pulled the nightgown over her head, the movement too quick for me to protest. She was wearing knickers and had her back to me so I had time to avert my eyes before I saw her breasts. I told her I'd be waiting on the landing, and left her alone.

She came out wearing blue jeans and a light grey woollen jumper. Moving past me, she continued towards her sister's door.

'What are you doing?' I asked.

'I want to see if Jane's awake. If she is, she can drive us.'

She knocked and opened the door. I saw a brief flash of two moving bodies, quickly covered by a duvet.

'Don't come in,' shouted Jane and Chloë quickly backed out.

I shook my head. 'Do you have a number for a taxi?'

The cab driver was a young woman, which surprised me. Chloë had found out where the nearest twenty-four-hour chemist was, and the driver told us it'd be fifteen pounds round trip. Chloë didn't flinch. We climbed into the taxi and had got as far as the local comprehensive when Chloë told the driver to stop.

'What?'

'It's my dad.'

'Where?'

'In the field.'

I assumed it was just the tiredness making her hallucinate, but I got out anyway and walked across to the field. And she was right, it was her father. He was squatting in a muddy ditch, naked apart from a pair of baggy white underpants and thick-lensed glasses. The moment he saw us he broke into a run.

'Rob,' Chloë called from inside the car.

'What?'

'Chase him.'

I looked at her dad's pale flabby figure disappearing into the darkness. 'No way. I'm not going out there on my own. What if he tries to attack me?'

'Rob, we have to get him home. He doesn't know what he's doing.'

'Look, he has to come home eventually. Let's leave him and go get my contact lens stuff.'

We walked back to the cab.

The taxi driver drove us to the all-night chemist. I'd been planning to claim they didn't have everything I needed, wanting to keep Chloë awake even longer, but the shop was surprisingly well stocked and after the incident with her dad I couldn't be bothered to lie. So I took the stuff up to the counter and Chloë paid for it. Her eyes looked even more sunken under the bright white light, and I wondered again about what was doing. I'd expected to find a persona naturally that would make this work for me, but maybe that was impossible. I still loved Chloë and found it so hard to hurt her, even if that was what she wanted and the only way to gain her respect. I knew she'd made me come here for a reason, and that it was something other than helping her father regain his sanity by remembering happier times. She'd made it clear that she was offering herself as a sacrifice for the inconvenience of coming here, but what I didn't understand was whether this was a temporary masochism or an attempt to bring us back together.

*

It was just after three when we got back inside the house. Chloë smiled weakly and started climbing the stairs. I caught her arm. 'I don't want to be in the lounge any more.'

'OK,' she said, 'let's move the camp-bed back upstairs.'

'No,' I told her, 'I want to sleep in your bed.'

'Rob . . .' she replied wearily, 'I need to stretch out. My back's so bad. If you're in my bed I really won't be able to move in the morning.'

'I'm sorry, Chloë, but that's what I want. You said I could ask for anything.'

Her head drooped and I followed her upstairs. She stopped outside her door. 'And you want to watch me undress?'

'No, I'll wait outside. Put your nightdress back on. Although take your knickers off this time.'

She called me when she was under the covers and I went in to join her in her long, narrow bed. The light was still on and she looked up at me before I started undressing.

'What are you going to sleep in?'

'Nothing.' I looked at her. 'Unless you want me to keep my pants on?'

She sighed. 'Would you mind?'

'No,' I replied, 'but why?'

'Take them off then, if you want to.'

'No, Chloë, it's OK. I don't want to make you uncomfortable.'

'Then don't get in my bed.'

I turned off the light, slipped off my socks, stripped to my underwear and slid in beside her. Chloë lay on her side, body clenched. I turned behind her, feeling the weight of my erection pressing against her buttocks. This seemed to release something inside Chloë, and in seconds she was sobbing with such violence that the only way I could combat her thrashing was to climb on top of her. Jack-knifing in agony, Chloë wailed so loudly I worried the rest of the house would think I was killing her.

'Chloë,' I shouted, 'please stop. I'm sorry, I'll get out. I didn't realise it would hurt so much.'

'It's not my back.'

'Then what is it?'

She kissed me. I hesitated, then pulled down my pants and lifted her nightdress, releasing her arms and rubbing my palm over her cunt. I wanted to finger her, but she was already pushing my hands away and arching for my cock.

I resisted stroking her bum as I fucked her, knowing how much she hated being touched there. I held her breasts instead, and wished, as I did every time, that there was more to sex than this. Chloë started fingering herself, and I fucked her as hard as I could, knowing that tonight we both needed something extreme, no matter how painful. I came at almost the exact same second she did, the shock of this causing us to squeeze each other, holding on so long that my muscles ached when I finally relaxed.

Then we slept.

Chloë woke me at eight. I asked her to skip work, but she said she couldn't. Then I asked her for a key.

'I'm sorry, I haven't had one cut for you yet.'

'But I'm meeting my girlfriend for lunch.'

She looked away. 'Mum's not working today. She can let you back in.'

I swallowed. 'Did your dad come home last night?'

'I don't think so.'

'Did you tell your mum about the field?'

'No she's worried enough already. That's why she's

staying home.'

'Chloë . . .'

'Yes?'

'Last night was incredible.'

'I'm sorry about that. I won't get so emotional next time. And you don't have to worry, I know you've got a girlfriend.'

I stayed in bed until ten, then went downstairs looking for food. Chloë's mum sat in the corner of the lounge, a large wooden board placed on top of the arms of her chair. She was drawing a picture of a rabbit eating a carrot.

'Hello, love, are you hungry?'

I nodded.

'There's cereal and fruit in the kitchen,' she told me. 'And bread if you want toast. But do you mind making it yourself?'

I shook my head and went into the kitchen, pouring myself a big bowl of cornflakes. I took a carton of juice from the fridge and filled a tall glass. Chloë's mum smiled at me as I came back into the lounge. Now, Chloë said you're having lunch with your girlfriend.'

'Yeah.'

'Do you have any idea what time you'll be back? Only I have to go to Sainsbury's at some point this afternoon and I want to make sure I'll be here to let you in.'

'I'm meeting Sally in Soho so it'll take a while, but I expect it'll be around four.'

'Four. OK. That should be fine, because even if I'm not here Erica and Jane should be back by then. Do you need me to buy anything particular for you?'

'I don't think so. If you're just doing a general shop . . .'

'Yes,' she said, 'I'll be getting food for everybody.'

'That's fine then.'

I sat on the settee opposite her, eating my cereal. Chloë's mum smiled as she worked on her drawing, tongue poking from the corner of her mouth.

'Have you and Chloë fucked yet?'

I put down my spoon. No point in lying. 'Yeah.'

She clapped her hands together. 'I knew it. Oh, it's so good for her. She gets so uptight. Can I ask you a question? Does Chloë like oral sex?'

'Um,' I said, squirming, 'we didn't have oral sex last night.'

'See, that's what I mean, if I hadn't had sex with someone in ages, the first thing I'd want is oral sex. I'm amazed Chloë can even get wet enough to fuck without being sucked first. There must've been some foreplay though, wasn't there?'

'A little bit of touching, but not much.' With that I tried to end the conversation, spooning more cereal into my mouth in silence.

'Rob?' she said finally.

'Yes?'

'Is there any chance you and Chloë might get back together? Be totally honest, I won't say anything to her one way or the other.'

'I don't think so,' I said, not wanting to say any more about it.

She nodded. 'OK.'

I finished my cornflakes and placed the bowl on the coffee table. 'What about you and Tony?'

'What about us?'

'Well, what's going to happen? Are you going to get a divorce?'

'God, no, I could never divorce Tony. He's the only man I've ever loved.'

'So what's going to happen?'

'He'll get back to normal eventually. In a way, I'm glad it's happening like this. I think I'd find it harder to cope if he was having a conventional mid-life crisis.'

'Do you and Tony still make love?'

'Of course.'

'Isn't it a bit scary when he doesn't speak?'

'A bit, but it's nowhere near as bad as when Chloë got like this. At least he's not doing himself any physical damage. The brain is a strange organ. And Tony's been getting in training for this ever since he was a little boy. All he's ever been interested in reading are books by mad people. I wouldn't exactly call what he's doing showing off, but you can trust me when I tell you there's a definite element of performance in his behaviour.'

She winked at me. I knew it was Chloë's dad who really deserved my anger, but the way Chloë's mum made herself so hopeless infuriated me. I went over to where she was sitting, taking her hand and forcing myself to look into her eyes, wanting to know whether it was excess guilt or an innate belief in her own virtue that made her so dangerous. She looked at me with the slightly goofy expression she affected in moments of high emotion, and I squeezed her hand. Fetching my jacket from the hallway, I left her to her drawing and walked out of the house.

'So how's your friend?' Sally asked me after we'd ordered.

'He's OK. I think it's a really good job I was there with him last night though. Thanks for letting me go.'

'Don't be silly. But I'm a bit worried about you, though. Are you sure you can cope with looking after this guy on your own?'

'Oh yeah,' I told her, 'he's a clever man. And he's

processing all of this breakdown stuff in a very rational, intellectual way.'

'And he's someone you know from university?' she asked, pushing me.

'Yeah. He's spent the last four years working on a Ph.D. that he's realised is totally useless, and he can't believe he's wasted so much of his life.'

'I'm sure it's not useless. Everyone feels like that at some point or other and it always turns out to be fine.'

'No, Sally, this is computer stuff. It's not like English or Philosophy where as long as you've got something to mark they give you a pass just for trying. This is something where he's found out that he's completely, categorically wrong.'

I watched Sally's mouth as she tried to process this. Sally was always so optimistic, and there was definitely something enjoyable about presenting her with insurmountable problems, especially if, as today, they were fictional. The sunlight was moving across her bare arms and I wondered what would happen if I told her the truth. She didn't know Chloë. They had never met and I didn't talk about her, but would she trust me with my ex-girlfriend? Of course, it was too late now I'd lied, especially as if she did get angry I'd have no way of knowing whether she was cross about the situation or the deceit, but she seemed so OK about me helping a male friend that I felt tempted to subject her to a harder test.

'Well,' said Sally, having considered the problem, 'in that case I suppose the important thing is to keep him distracted.'

I got back to Chloë's house later than I'd expected. Her mum was still at the supermarket so I sat in the lounge with Erica and Jane.

'Erica,' I asked, 'did Chloë's parents pay you for that painting?'

'Yeah,' Jane answered for her, 'fifty pounds. My dad says art should always be paid for.'

'So I could pay you to do a similar one for me?'

Erica shook her head. 'I don't do that sort of art any more.'

We were all distracted by a sudden loud banging against the patio doors. Looking up, the three of us were confronted by Chloë's father, naked and covered in mud, using his curled fists to hammer on the glass.

'Oh fuck,' said Jane.

We got him upstairs and into the bath before Chloë's mum came home. I didn't want to leave him alone with razor blades and water, but the two girls told me I was being silly and dragged me downstairs.

'Dad's home,' Jane told her mum as she came through the door carrying three plastic bags.

'Great. Can you help me with the shopping?'

We trooped outside and brought everything in. Being here without Chloë made me feel claustrophobic, and I hoped she would come home soon.

When Chloë's father reappeared, he was wearing a smart suit and looking perfectly normal. I wondered whether he realised it was early evening, or if he'd put on these clothes because he thought it was time to go to work. Remembering what Chloë's mum had said about how me coming back would make him normal again, I decided to ignore his weirdness and force him into a conversation.

'Hey, Tony, I've been meaning to tell you, I've seen loads of films you recommended to me.'

He smiled, but didn't reply.

'And I've seen loads of new films that I'm sure you'll like. But the main film I really think you should see is *The Insider*. Russell Crowe's character is just like you.'

The way he squirmed made me realise I was almost shouting at him, as if he was ninety instead of fifty-three. I'd also adopted a cheeky, patronising tone, drawing surprised glances from the rest of the family. Not wanting to upset them, I left Tony to his sulk and went upstairs to Chloë's bedroom.

I moved around the room, looking through her drawers, flicking through her tapes. She didn't seem to have bought anything new since we'd broken up. I looked along the row of cases, feeling sad and nostalgic. *Scott 1, 2 3* and *4. Tilt.* The first *Pavement* album. *Kate Bush. Blood, Sweat and Tears. Smashing Pumpkins.* A copy of *Hot Buttered Soul* inscribed by her ex, Lucien, to 'a hot buttered Chloë'. I pulled it out and read the blue biro writing again, surprised it still made me sick with jealousy. I did not hear her as she entered the room.

Chloë looked at me.

'How come you didn't call him?' I asked her.

'Who?'

'Lucien. I thought he was your one true love.'

She didn't say anything, instead coming across and taking the tape from me. 'Do you want to listen to this?'

I shook my head. 'I want you to tell me about them.'

'Who?'

'The two guys. The ones you slept with after breaking up with me.'

'It's not important.'

'Yes it is. You broke up with me because you said you'd started fancying other men.'

'And?'

'And I want to know if you did anything about it. I want to know if you met those guys while you were going out with me.'

'Why are you like this?'

'Like what?'

'So relentless.'

I didn't have an answer, instead I lay down on the bed and beckoned for her to join me. She was crying now, in a less dramatic, more resigned way than yesterday, her arms hanging limp. I let her lie beside me on her tiny bed.

'Your dad came back.'

'I know. Mum wants us to come downstairs for dinner.'

'I tried to make him speak.'

She laughed at my jokey, deliberately high-pitched tone, and looked up at me from beneath her fringe. 'Were you successful?'

'No.'

'I love you, Rob.'

'I love you too.'

She smiled and we adjusted ourselves on the mattress. 'Chloë?'

'Yes?'

'Do you want me to leave my girlfriend?'

'I couldn't ask you to do that.'

'You could.'

'No, I mean, I couldn't. I wouldn't be able to give you what you want in return.'

I sat up, exasperated. 'Why do you think everyone's always making demands on you?'

'You are making demands on me. You say you're not now, but you know what would happen if we got back together.'

'Fucking forget it, then. I'm sorry I even offered. You're a stupid, selfish bitch.'

She started crying again. 'I'm not, I'm not, everyone's always saying that and it's so unfair . . . I'm doing everything I can . . . for everyone . . . don't you think I'd love to have you back? Don't you think I want that more than anything?'

'Then ask me to leave my girlfriend.'

'I can't, Rob, I can't. If I made you do that you could, you could . . .'

'I could what?'

'You could kill me.'

We went downstairs for dinner. Jane and Erica were already at the table. Chloë's mum was in the kitchen, while her dad sat in his chair in the corner of the lounge, reading a newspaper.

'Does he know it's dinnertime?' I whispered to Jane.

He looked up, put down the paper, and came across to the table. Jane's fingers were purple.

'What happened?'

She examined her hand. 'Oh, I've been dying stuff. For Erica's new project.'

Chloë's mum carried the first two plates in from the kitchen and placed them in front of the two girls.

'Oh,' I said, looking up at her, 'I don't eat baked beans.'

'I know,' she said, 'and you haven't got beans, you've got steak. That's just for those two.'

I looked at their identically arranged dinners and decided it was some kind of art world thing. Chloë took my hand beneath the table and I brushed my fingers across her thigh, trying to tactilely apologise for our argument.

*

'I wish I didn't love the way you dress so much,' I said to Chloë after dinner, when we were back upstairs and lying again on her bed.

She smiled at me and I tugged up her skirt. 'I mean, I love that you wear suspenders, and I know that's wrong. You're the only girlfriend I've had who's ever worn them, and I know you like them, and wear them only for yourself because you don't like tights, but still, it seems so wrong,' I ran my fingers up over her thighs, 'that I like them so much.'

She turned and kissed me. 'I don't mind. I want you to like the way I dress.'

'Your mum was asking me all sorts of personal questions about you today.'

'Oh God, what . . .'

I moved down so I was facing her cunt, then slowly tugged down her knickers.

'She was asking me if you liked oral sex.'

'Oh God, she's so disgusting.'

Chloë fell asleep afterwards, having got such little rest the previous night. I felt much more goodwill towards her than I had yesterday and decided to let her have the bed to herself. I didn't really fancy going downstairs to pick up my camp-bed, but I got through the process quickly by enlisting Erica's help. I still didn't feel that sleepy so I searched Chloë's drawers for something to read, not surprised when I discovered she'd been lying about no longer keeping a diary.

I awoke at two o'clock the following afternoon. Feeling groggy, I went to the bathroom and drank from the tap, not caring which tank the water came from. Then I returned to

Chloë's bedroom, put on pants and a T-shirt and went downstairs. I was going out to the kitchen for some proper breakfast when I noticed Tony. He was lying in the garden, face down in the grass. His body was slumped, but he didn't look dead. He seemed to be reaching for something just out of his grasp, but putting little effort into it. I don't know why I freaked, I just suddenly saw myself still here in three years' time, still trying to sort out this family. I wasn't man enough for this, no matter how much I still loved Chloë. If I didn't go now, I would never have such a perfect opportunity. So I went upstairs, removed the painting from above her parents' bed, fetched my purple sportsbag, and left.

Facing the Music

ANNA DAVIS

'Aren't you taking your Walkman?'

I freeze, with my hand on the front-door handle. I'm almost gone and I'm frustratingly close to being gone, but in fact I'm still here. I let my hand fall away from the door, curling my fingers into my palm so she won't see the purple Hard Candy nail varnish. I must turn around and speak to her. I must look her straight in the eye and my face must show nothing. Better not smile – a smile would be the most suspicious expression of all.

I turn. Mum is standing at the top of the stairs, hands on hips. Her face looks all wrong, somehow. As though she, too, is trying to look me straight in the eye and show nothing of what she is thinking.

'What?'

'I said, aren't you taking your Walkman?'

'No. I've got to start on my revision. Biology.'

I delve into the canvas bag I'm carrying over my

shoulder and pull out my Biology textbook to show her, hoping as I do so that she won't notice the nail varnish.

'But you always take your Walkman.'

'No, I don't. Not when I have other stuff to do. Anyway, *ER*'s on later. I'll do some revision and I'll watch *ER*.'

'Oh.'

The textbook droops in my hand. I shove it back in the bag.

She scrapes her hair behind her ears, even though it was behind her ears to start with, and she keeps staring at me, through me. I've blown it. I was a fool to think I could outsmart her, but it was all going so well. The phone call I made to Mum from Sarah's house was the riskiest bit, but I knew I could pull that off. I do a perfect Jemima Thrower impression – the way she drawls and drags out her vowels, those little clicking noises she makes sucking on her teeth. Afterwards I worried that the *real* Jemima Thrower would ring up and ask if I could babysit on Thursday. But that didn't happen.

No, in the end it is the bloody Walkman that has scuppered me. I had the bag, I had the schoolbooks – but I forgot the Walkman. And a worse mistake – I didn't go back for it when she caught me out. Maybe I could still go back for it . . . no, it's too late now.

'Do you think you'll be home late?' she asks.

'Don't know.' Trouble is, I have to go on with this, even though she's caught me out. My only alternative is to confess. And then I would have to take a bollocking without having done anything worth being bollocked for.

'Right. Well . . . I hope they won't keep you too late. It is a school night, after all.'

'Mum!' calls my brother Jake, from the kitchen. 'Mum, can you come here? The sauce won't go thick.'

Momentary distraction. Her bout of intense staring is over and my chance has come. I seize it.

'Bye then, Mum.' My purple-tipped fingers are on the door handle and I'm away.

Outside the air is crisp, bracing. I pull my hands inside the sleeves of my leather jacket and walk quickly, purposefully, the stiletto heels of my new boots tap-tapping on the paving stones. There's a thrill ripping through my chest and making me want to whoop. I've done it after all – I've got out! In celebration of my own ingenuity I do this thing that I sometimes do which is like hugging yourself from the inside. I am Skill. Dodging the big puddle at the corner of Teilo Street I turn right on to Cathedral Road and head down to the bus stop.

The dingy metal shelter stinks of piss so I stand out on the pavement, looking up at the stars to kill time and trying to pick out the shapes of constellations, while cars flash by into town. Some of them honk their horns at me, at my legs. I look great in my excellent new boots. I wonder if Sean will notice them and pay me a compliment. I bet he will.

Sean Porter is the fantastic singer and front man of Citizen Duane, the best band in Cardiff. They're playing tonight at the Clwb Ifor Bach in town. Sean is good friends with our next-door neighbours, Chris and Marie, and I first saw Citizen Duane two months ago when they played at Marie's thirtieth birthday party at the Pontcanna Electricity Club. Since then I have seen them play seventeen times. Sometimes I take my best friend Lucy with me but she isn't always allowed to go out, so more often than not I end up going on my own. The first time I did this I was scared they would think I was some sort of desperate groupie and I wore my combats and a jumper so I wouldn't be too tarty and noticeable. Chris, the PA guy, was very nice to me that night – he bought me a drink and let me sit with him at the sound desk, so in fact I didn't feel like a sad groupie at all. Chris is a bit sleazy and he stinks of BO but he's all right. And since then I've got to know the guys really well, so now it's like I'm one of them.

Mum's pretty good about letting me go out at the weekends as long as I'm home by midnight, but she won't let me go out on school nights. She says this is because I will be tired in school the next day. But if that's true, why does she let me go babysitting for the Throwers? I'm just as late when I've been babysitting as I am when I go out to see Citizen Duane, so what's the bloody difference, that's what I want to know?

The shit hit the fan when I wanted to go and see Citizen Duane play at TJ's in Newport last Tuesday. This was due to be a great gig. TJ's is where Catatonia and Super Furry Animals used to play before they got famous, not to mention The Manics. And Sean said they were expecting an A&R man from Creation Records to come along, though apparently he didn't turn up in the end. The gig would be over by 11 p.m. and Sean said they'd give me a lift home in the van so there shouldn't have been a problem but Mum wasn't having any of it. We had a massive row and she screamed at me that it's just not fair that she has to do all the disciplining of her kids while my dad gets to swan in and out and have us for nice easy holidays, and how it isn't appropriate for fifteen-year-old girls to be gadding about with grown men in pubs. I think that's pretty rich, since there is clearly no problem with fifteen-year-old girls looking after their twelve-year-old brothers while their mothers are away at stupid conferences in places like Milton Keynes and Durham for three or four days at a time. I'm just not prepared to miss any more Citizen Duane gigs.

Shit – there's a red Nissan turning out of Teilo Street. Mum! I hope to God she hasn't seen me. I shrink back into the bus shelter, hiding myself from view. Oh, Christ, she's pulling up on the other side of the road and winding down her window. 'Jane? Is that you in there?'

Slowly, I shuffle out of the bus shelter and cross the road to her car. I have no idea what I am going to say to her. The Throwers only live five minutes' walk away in the opposite direction so there is no reason whatsoever for me to be standing at this bus stop.

She leans over and opens the passenger door. 'Get in.'

'Hi, Mum. Where are you going?'

'Where am *I* going? What were you doing in that bus shelter, Jane?'

'An old woman asked me the time. I just stopped to tell her.'

'Where is she now?'

'Gone.'

She is looking at me as though I am insect-life or something. She sighs and pushes her hair behind her ears. 'Jane, I want you to tell me the truth. Where are you really going?'

'You know where I'm going. Babysitting. At the Throwers.'

'Right.' Her voice is strained, tense with suppressed anger. 'I'll give you a lift, then.'

'Fine. Thanks.'

She starts the engine and pulls out into the traffic. My heart is going thud-thud. If the Throwers lived further away I'd have time to think of a plan. As it is they only live on Llandaff Road and we're there in about half a minute. Mum parks just outside the front gate to the Wishing Well, which is what they call their house. Her face looks all hollow, as though she's gritting her teeth and sucking her cheeks in. It would be a good idea to lean over and give her a kiss, but I can't bring myself to do it. Instead, I open the door and clamber out on to the pavement.

'Wearing your new boots, I see,' comments Mum drily.

'Thanks for the lift, Mum. Bye.' I slam the door and give her a little wave. But she's not moving. I remain standing there for what feels like forever. Still she's not moving. She's just sitting there, staring at me. She presses the button to open the passenger window.

'I'll just wait for you to go inside,' she says.

'There's no need, Mum.'

'Yes, there is.'

'OK. Thanks. Bye.'

I turn and fumble with the gate catch. My fingers are sweaty. Mum just sits there watching me. She must be absolutely loving this. For the second time I am tempted to abandon this stupid plan, go back to the car and confess. But then I think about Sean hitting the high note in the song 'In That Light', the sheer jubilation in his face. And I think about how sad he was at their gig in Barry last weekend. When I asked him what was wrong, he told me that Carol, his girlfriend of five years, had walked out on him that morning and taken the cat. He sang with a real passion that night, a passion sprung from deep pain.

I must go on with this. There must still be a way to pull it off.

Closing the gate behind me I start to climb the twisting stone steps that lead steeply up to the house, past Jemima's row of bonsai and miniature ferns, through the ornate rockery, past the well itself, and beneath the shade of the willow tree which Mike is thinking of having chopped down to improve the light in their living room.

Arriving at the front door, I peer down at Mum. She's still there, sitting, waiting. I ring the bell – can't see that I have a choice – and stand about, trying to work out what to say to Jemima and Mike. The lamps are on in the living room and I can hear the telly so at least they're in. After a moment there are footsteps in the hall and the light is switched on.

'Hello, Jane.' Jemima has had a new perm. It's way too bouffant. She's smiling at me in a confused sort of way. 'What are you doing here?'

'Hi, Jemima. I *am* supposed to be babysitting for you tonight, aren't I?'

'No, I don't think so.' Her smile is still firmly in place. It's her basic expression to use on tradesmen and the like. I'm a sort of tradesman, in a way. She sucks on her teeth making one of those clicking noises, and says, 'I'm afraid you've made a mistake.'

'Oh. I'm really sorry.'

'That's quite all right, Jane. See you next Tuesday.'

She actually starts to close the door on me, so I give a sort of squeak.

'Jemima, could I come in for a moment? Please?'

'Of course.' She opens the door again and moves aside to let me past. She's wearing her silly fluffy mules. I don't look down to see Mum drive away but I give myself another of those inner hugs.

Mike is in the living room, watching football on Sky and sipping something that looks like whisky in a fancy glass. He switches the TV off when I come in. Julia and Robin have already been put to bed, thank God.

'Hello there, Jane. To what do we owe this pleasure?'

He's always like that. Friendly but in a patronising way. I don't like him. He's got a big face which is very ugly.

Jemima once told me he had plastic surgery on his jaw a few years ago and had to wear a frame around his head for weeks. She said it made him look like Davros. Apparently the surgery isn't permanent and he'll have to have more in a year or two to stop his jaw from collapsing. If this ugly face is the end result of the surgery, he must have been absolutely *hideous* before.

'Jane thought she was babysitting for us tonight,' explains Jemima.

'I see,' says Mike. 'Would you like a drink, Jane? Bacardi and Coke?'

'Yes, please.'

Mike goes out to the kitchen to fix my drink, leaving me alone with Jemima. She is giving me a very searching look. I think those sort of looks are a mother thing.

'So, Jane,' she says softly. 'What's really going on, then?'

Shit. Scuppered again. The urge to confess is intense. But if I tell her, she will send me home, for sure, and Mum will bollock me. Sean said on the phone yesterday that he wants me to sing backing vocals tonight for their cover version of 'Take Me to the River'. I did that last weekend when they played in Barry and it was fantastic. Standing up on stage next to Sean, knowing that every girl in the room was jealous of me. Sean says my harmonies are really great. If I don't turn up, he might ask someone else to come up on the stage instead. I couldn't bear that.

'Sorry, Jemima. I didn't really think I was babysitting tonight. But I had a row with my mother and I just had to get out and have a walk to calm down. I sort of found myself outside your house and I wanted to come and sit in your lovely living room and talk to you. You're always so nice to me. So understanding.'

'Poor poppet.' Jemima looks all melty. 'You were

absolutely right to come here, wasn't she, Mike?'

'Absolutely,' says Mike, putting a glass in my hand.

I sit sipping my Bacardi and Coke and somehow I manage to have a conversation with them about Robin's problems with Maths and Julia's swimming certificate. But all the time I'm thinking about how I'm going to dance like a wild animal when Citizen Duane play 'Psychic Sisters', and how everyone in the room is going to look at me. The upstairs bar of the Clwb Ifor Bach is excellent for dancing. And then I'm draining the dregs of my drink and saying, 'I feel so much better now. Thanks *so* much.'

'It's a pleasure,' says Mike, smiling his ugly smile.

'Sorry to be rude, but would it be OK if I give my Mum a quick call to tell her I'm on my way back?'

'Of course, Jane,' says Jemima. 'You know where it is.'

The phone is out in the hall. I close the living room door so they won't be able to hear what I'm saying. Then I dial the number, and wait while the phone at home rings three times.

'Hello?'

'Hi, Jake, it's me.'

'Jane! What's going on?'

'Nothing. I'm babysitting at Jemima and Mike's house. Is Mum there?'

'No. She came in and started going all weird. She was crying and stuff. She's gone next door now to talk to Chris and Marie.'

'Shit!'

'What have you done, Jane?'

'Nothing. Listen, Jake, when Mum comes back tell her I phoned from the Throwers' house to see if she was all right. But tell her she can't call me back because when the phone rings here it wakes the kids up. OK?'

'OK, Jane. Jane . . .'

'I've got to go now, Jake. Bye.'

The living room door is opening as I'm replacing the receiver and Jemima is coming out.

'Is everything all right, Jane?'

'Oh, yes, fine. I feel much better now and I've told Mum I'm coming straight home.'

She looks so happy at having been the peacemaker. She puts a hand on my shoulder and I can just tell she's about to give me some woman-to-woman advice.

'You know, Jane, your mother has a lot on her plate,' she drawls. 'I expect she finds it hard sometimes – being on her own and having such a demanding job. And I expect that sometimes she says things she doesn't mean to say, things she might regret saying afterwards.'

'She's not on her own. She has me and Jake.'

'But she doesn't have your father with her, does she?' Jemima gives my cheek a little stroke. This really bugs me.

'Yeah, well, thanks for the drink and the chat. I've got to get back now or she'll be worried.'

She nods, goes to open the front door for me. 'Off you go then, Jane. And remember – try to be patient with your mother. She loves you.'

'Yeah, I know. Bye.'

Pukesville.

I wish my stilettos didn't make such a loud tap-tapping on the pavement. Stealth is essential. I should never have made that phone call. It was a major mistake. Jake is useless at this sort of thing, and when he tells Mum not to call me at the Throwers', that is, of course, the very first thing she will do. I am now destined to receive a huge bollocking and to lose my regular babysitting job for being generally untrustworthy and a liar. But I am determined to have a night worth the punishment. I must get to that gig without being sprung.

Bus stops are too risky. The Nissan will be cruising the streets any time now and I do not want to be a sitting duck. Neither can I walk up Cathedral Road, which is the main route into town and therefore dangerous. Instead I choose to turn right along Llandaff Road, heading into the back streets of Canton. It'll take me a long time to weave my way through this maze of terraced housing and cobbles but I'll still get to the Clwb Ifor Bach long before the band are due to start playing.

I'm tap-tapping my way down some tiny road that looks like every other road around here. The new boots are rubbing my toes a bit. I'm singing to myself inside my head to keep my spirits up – Citizen Duane's new song, 'Bumpy Ride'. Trying to remember the words. Can't remember much because I've only heard it twice but it keeps coming back to this one cool line – 'Making Love in an Easier Position'. I wonder if Sean wrote the song about Carol. Smelly Chris, the PA guy, told me Sean's been sleeping with someone else but I don't believe him. Sean wouldn't do that to Carol – not now she's having his baby. He truly loves her and was gutted when she left him last week.

The end of the road. Left or right now? I don't know which way town is from here but I choose left. It's so quiet down these narrow terraced streets. Hardly any cars. The only noises are the sounds of people's tellies. There are very few street lights and I pick my way across the cracked paving stones by the light from people's living rooms. It forces its way through the slats in blinds and the gaps between closed curtains. I'm a bit lost, to tell the truth. And a bit spooked. There's a bloke walking up the street towards me who's all hunched over and muttering to himself. Probably pissed. He'd better not give me any trouble or I'll kick him where it hurts with my stilettos. Ah, he's turning into the alley. Good. But wait a minute . . . Ugh, he's having a waz in the alley and it's trickling down into the road in a long stream. I feel nervous about having to walk past the opening to the alley while he's still wazzing away.

'Hello, darling. Where are you off to, all tarted up like that? Who's the lucky bloke, then?'

'Fuck off.'

I quicken my pace, leaving him far behind. Mum would go mad if she knew I was walking around here on my own.

I've been walking for over half an hour now and my feet are killing me, but at least I know where I am. This is Kings Road. It will take me out on to Cowbridge Road East and straight into town. I am only ten minutes' walk away from the Clwb Ifor Bach, ten minutes away from Sean. I feel safer too – there are more people around here, going in and out of the Kings Castle pub and down to the curry houses.

There's a sudden glare of headlights swinging towards me . . . A red car . . . A Nissan? No, it's a Toyota. Thank Christ! My thumping heart quietens down again.

A phone box . . . Perhaps I'll just give a quick call to Jake. Find out what's happening. After all, there's no point in my jumping a mile and a half in the air every time a red car goes by if Mum's safe at home, is there? If she answers I'll just hang up. I grope in the canvas bag for some change and swing into the box.

'Hello?'

'Jake, it's me.'

'Jane! Where are you? Mum's going mental!'

'What's happening, Jake?'

'Are you at that Sean's house?'

'No, of course not. I'm in a phone box.'

'She says you're absolutely besotted with him. She went hunting for your address book to find out where he lives but she couldn't find it. Then she went round to Chris and Marie's again to ask them but they wouldn't tell her. They said Sean wouldn't do anything like that but Mum won't believe them.'

'Where's Mum now?'

'She says you're having an affair with him. Are you having an affair with him, Jane?'

'God, how stupid, of course I'm not! Look, I'm nearly out of money. Where's Mum now?'

'I don't know. She drove off in the car. She won't stop crying . . . Jane, when are you coming home? I'm scared.'

'Don't be a twat, Jake. When Mum gets back just tell her . . . Tell her there's no need to worry about me. Tell her I'm sorry.'

'When are you coming home, Jane?'

'Later.'

I slam the phone down just as my money is about to run out.

Town. Buzzy and exciting. I'm crossing the bridge over the River Taff, passing the castle which is all pretty and orange in the floodlights, looking up at the Welsh dragon fluttering on its flag pole high above. I feel as though this place is full to bursting with moments I haven't lived yet. Not even my mother is going to stop me from living them. And now I'm turning off the main drag, ducking down the seedy alleyway which leads to the Clwb Ifor Bach, to Sean. Arriving at the scruffy little door. Knocking. Waiting. Knocking again.

'Hello, darling, what can I do for you?'

It's the bald bouncer with the funny eye. He only opens the door a crack, as though there's something really secret going on inside that I mustn't see. They're like that here because it's the Welsh club. They only let non-Welsh speakers like me in when there's a gig on upstairs. And there's always the same bunch of blokes in the downstairs bar with their pints of SA, giving it all the yakky yakky and giving us dirty looks as we go up.

'I've come for the Citizen Duane gig. I guess I'm a bit early.'

'I should say you are.' He just stands there, looking at my legs, blinking, doing nothing.

'Well, can I come in or do I have to come back later?'

'Come back next week, babes.'

'What?'

'They cancelled, love. Didn't you see the sign?'

He opens the door just wide enough to stick his arm out and point at a blackboard under the window, headed 'Clwb Ifor Bach 2000'. On it is chalked: 'Wednesday 5th April – Citizen Duane gig postponed due to sore throat. Will now take place Thursday 13th April'.

'But they can't just cancel. They can't!'

'Sorry, babes, it's out of my control. You wanna take it up with that poncy singer.'

And the door bangs shut in my face.

Facing the door. Reading the words on the blackboard over and over. Despair. Deepest despair like I've never known before. There's a real physical pain behind my ribs. There will be no dancing, no music, no dreaming tonight. There will only be a bollocking.

Somewhere in this shitty town my mother is driving around in a frenzy, imagining I am in bed with Sean Porter.

The very idea makes me blush – that she could think this of me and of him. It is all so far from reality.

But here I am being totally selfish when something is clearly very wrong with Sean. He's sung gigs with sore throats before. Jesus, he's sung with infected tonsils and a fever. He would never cancel a gig for something this trivial. The more I think about it the more worried I am. He was in such a state about Carol last week . . .

I find a piss-stinking phone box on St Mary Street and shove a pound coin – the only coin I have left in my purse – in the slot. I know Sean's number off by heart because I call him several times a week to find out about gigs. He's always so helpful, so friendly.

'Hello?' It's a woman's voice.

'Hi . . . who's that?'

'It's Carol. Who is this, please?'

'Oh. Hi, Carol. It's Jane.'

'Jane?'

'Yes. Jane who comes to see the band.'

'Oh, right. Jane . . . Hang on a second. I'll give Sean a shout. He was in the shower but I think he's out now.'

'No, no. Don't disturb him. There's no need. I . . . I just wanted to make sure he's OK. You know, the sore throat.'

'Sore throat? Oh yeah, right . . . He's fine, Jane. They're playing next Thursday at the Clwb Ifor Bach. Maybe I'll see you there?'

'Yeah, maybe. Thanks, Carol.'

'No problem. I'll tell him you called.'

I replace the receiver shakily. He's fine. Sean is fine. And he's back with Carol. This is good news, isn't it?

Well, if he's fine, why did he cancel the bloody gig? The git!

I come out of the phone box on to the street. Look

around me at the casino over the road. At the Irish pub, the bars, the girls in short dresses, the couples arm in arm. There's so much life here and none of it is mine. In front of me a line of taxis is waiting at the rank. In a moment or two I will get into the front one and tell the driver to take me home to Teilo Street, Pontcanna. Home for my bollocking. I will be bollocked as hard as I've ever been bollocked before but I will survive because I am strong. I only wish I had actually done something worth being bollocked for. Jesus, I've never even kissed anyone properly. Not with tongues.

I'll just stand here for a couple of minutes, watching the world I am not a part of, before I get into that taxi. Give myself a hug from the inside. God knows I need a hug from someone. I'll take just a moment or two for myself. And then I'll go home to Mum and Jake. Home to face the music.

Three Love Stories

BO FOWLER

The Pretty Librarian

I was getting a book out of the library, *The Sirens of Titan* by Kurt Vonnegut, and I handed it over to this very pretty librarian who said something like, 'Oh Kurt Vonnegut, he came here last year.'

I told her he was my idol, that if I could write a tenth as well as him I'd be happy.

That's what I said and it's true.

I asked her how many books I could take out.

Fifteen.

A few days later I am visiting this other girl I met, she wears White Musk and has this funny neck I haven't decided if I like or not. I'm trying to find this girl with the funny neck's room. I said I'd take her out to dinner, but she's given me the wrong number or I took it down wrong. I wrote down room K212 but some guy Andrew had his name on the door to room K212. I have this terrible idea that Andrew might be the girl with the funny neck's boyfriend.

I knock anyway. Andrew isn't in.

I try the floor below. Nope, no one has heard of a girl called Emma, the girl with the funny neck I'm not sure I like or not.

Then I try upstairs.

Emma is in the doorway of room K213, she's putting on these big boots. Her friends are getting ready to go out. She says, 'We're going to the pub, want to come?' I say, 'Sure.' Her neck's still funny.

It's really packed and I queue for hours at the bar. I'm bored queuing so I just say for a joke to this girl who's in front of me, 'Perhaps in another life we were complete strangers.'

I'm always saying that.

And she says, 'Perhaps in another life you could write one tenth as well as Kurt Vonnegut.'

It's the pretty librarian.

We talked about art and law. She did a degree in French, Japanese and business studies, she's a cradle Catholic.

At the end of the evening she gets on her bike and leaves me in a part of town I don't know.

When I get home I go straight to bed. I try to masturbate about the pretty librarian, but even though she was very pretty I can't. Sometimes you just can't masturbate about pretty women. So I masturbate about Emma.

Were We Married?

I met this girl I hadn't seen since school in a bar. We talked about things. She had more spots than before. Her boyfriend was a sculptor. One thing we talked about was a play we'd both been in. We couldn't remember if, in the play, I had been her husband or not. We said things like, 'Were we married? I can't remember, it's been so long.'

I hope someone heard us talking like that.

The Girlfriend

I was seeing this girl who was kind of odd, she had pen nibs instead of nipples.

During sex she'd write things in blue all over my duvet. The first night she wrote *The ironsmith fashions it and works it over the coals, he shapes it with hammers and forges it with his strong arm; he becomes hungry and his strength fails, he drinks no*

Then, the second night she wrote *water and is faint. The carpenter stretches a line, he marks it out with a pencil: he fashions it with planes, and marks it with a compass; he shapes it into the figure of a man, and with the beauty of a man, to dwell in a house. He cuts down cedars; or he chooses a holm tree or an oak and lets it grow strong among the trees*

I couldn't tell if she did it on purpose or not. She said she wasn't aware of it. It cost me a fortune in dry-cleaning bills.

Anyway, we stopped going out when she came over one day and found *of the forest; he plants a cedar and the rain nourishes it. Then it becomes fuel for a man; he takes part of it and warms himself, he kindles a fire and bakes bread; also he makes a god and worships it. Half of it he burns in the fire; over the other half he eats flesh, he roasts meat and is satisfied; also he warms himself and says* written on my duvet. It was in red. Her sister had written it.

Monkey See

MATTHEW BRANTON

March

He looked at people getting it on all day and hadn't got one
on for his wife in four months. Not while she was there,
anyway.

He had a list like a film censor – a table he'd knocked up
in ClarisWorks at home – that ran to six sides of A4. One
pile of each page filled a six-shelf tray next to the PC: top
shelf for couples, second for threes, third for fours-&-mores,
fourth for pain, fifth for toileting, ground floor for children
and animals. He ordered it that way based on the frequency
of what he saw, so that the most frequently used sheets were
on the top. He meant no pecking order by it.

He'd had to draw up the lists himself because no one had
done this job before him. He was the only one in the nick
who knew much about PCs so he got it. The PC in front
of him only had room to run Quicktime these days and the
printer beneath his desk had taken one scuff too many. The
lists he'd had to do at home had been xeroxed so many

times the gridlines looked like they'd been drawn in his step-daughter, Lori's eyeliner. The pen in his left hand moved up and down the boxes as his right hand clicked.

DI Sturgess put his head over the partition and said, 'Derek, mate.'

'Two secs,' he muttered, not looking up.

Sturgess glanced at the screen, turned his mouth down and ducked back.

Fran rang before lunch, told him to pay the gas. The bill had come in that morning and there was a £7.50 credit for prompt payment. She told him to make sure he did it before he left. He asked about her day and she said her team leader was trying to do her head in.

It brightened up in the afternoon and he had to swivel his screen away from the low sun, turn his cuffs back over his freckled forearms. He was working down a stack of page twos, a rush-job – the case against the hard-drive's owner had to go to the CPS by the end of next week, the sticky had said – and he stroked six boxes with his pen even as he hit control-W, revealing the picture behind the one he'd just ticked off.

His eyes shifted focus and saw a woman taking one man in her mouth and another up her front – what he'd come to term a spit-roast – squatting on one with his feet towards the camera: he'd named this the cross-bow, because if you drew it with stick figures it looked like one. He checked the box on page two labelled SR and the box labelled CB, ran his eye over the other options to see if any applied: did any of the participants appear to be under eighteen? No. Were any of the male organs unusually large? And if so, was there pain involved in the penetration? Borderline. The guy underneath had a girth on him, no barney there: but the girl was looking up at the bloke she was blowing, which suggested – to Derek at least – that she was maybe halfway into it. He left the box blank. Was the grouping mixed race? Possibly – the girl looked a bit like Jennifer Lopez, and he wrote '*F-PR?*' in the box next to the I/R designation. I/R meant inter-racial, PR, Puerto Rican. Since most of it came from the States he'd learned a lot about the ethnic mix there, saw it himself last September in Florida. Pointed them all out to Fran, not that she'd been interested. She'd said she didn't want him bringing his work home but he'd had a sense there was more to it than that.

He remembered the gas as the tea-trolley came round. He got a custard danish that had sat around too long and a cup of builder's, ate the cake while he waited on hold for the bank. The girl who eventually answered was Manc, though the bank was in Leeds: he gazed vacantly at a woman with a wolfhound while the Manc girl took him through security. He couldn't remember his memorable fact – it was usually his mother's maiden name or his first wife's birthday – and he had to ask for a hint and then think hard for a moment to get it.

He never knew whose computers he was checking. Most of the time, he was aware, they were just looking for leverage: *had a look on your hard disk, Short-eyes: you can talk to us or you can talk to Vice and I'll tell you for nothing, you don't wanna talk to Vice.* Fraud collar, he bet, silly sods. He didn't have to be told to know: fraud was the growth industry, and the hardest to pin without some help from the suspect. So 14-gig tapes piled up through the internal mail; he took one off the top every morning, set it to upload onto his own, 20-gig drive, and picked up a butterscotch-with-sprinkles from the canteen while it was spooling. He liked to get his breakfast down before he started.

There were several ways to do it. He could run the Yank app. that looked for picture files, then check those files for the percentage of flesh-tone pixels: but too low a setting picked up holiday snaps, too high missed the latex and leather, or the close-ups. It took ten minutes just to pull files for you and crashed your machine more often than not. He hardly ever used it.

Better was to search for file names that would lead to the folder you were looking for. Hardly anyone was stupid enough to leave filetype identifiers on the end – .jpg, .rm, .mov – and most of the time they renamed them completely, so you searched for naming systems. BJ was always a good start. CS for come-shot, or MS for money. FCL. DP. WS. Eight times out of ten you got a result.

If you didn't, you had to work harder, try and think like them. People kept it buried in their hard drives, usually the system folder, in his experience, where there were thousands of plug-ins and extensions to lose their collection amongst. But they wanted to get at it fast when the urge was on them: at the fag-end of the day, when the wife had gone to bed scowling about work; when they were lonely and tired and needed to feel like part of the human race again. They didn't want to be opening a dozen folders to find the good stuff, so there was usually a shortcut near the surface that would take you in deep: a folder alias hidden behind a document icon was a common one. You had to get a feel for the way they liked to organise; then think like them, say to yourself *where would I put it, if this was mine, if this was what I needed?*

He'd got good at it, hit paydirt inside two minutes almost always. He was only meant to be doing it for three months to begin with, but no one else in the nick had any talent for it. Three months turned to six, then to nine, now to fourteen. He heard the uniform call him Bitchfinder General around the canteen till he put a stop to it. He was proud to be good at his job but once you'd found the stash the rest was monkey work. Open the pix, tick the boxes: monkey see, monkey do. He knocked off at five-thirty while the uniform went through till seven. Who was the monkey there?

He took the commuter train home, had to pull his warrant card every few months or so – pissed-up city boys, school kids with screwdrivers, office girls getting humped in the toilet. One asked if he wanted to join in once, cheeky tart. She didn't know he'd been on the slack since three weeks after the computer detail started. Fran did, but she'd got it all wrong. Did she want this marriage to work, after her last one? Yes, she did. Did she want him back in uniform? No, she didn't. He loved her, but she broke his bollocks sometimes.

He walked home from the station, mile and two clicks by his dashboard clock and he needed every step. Fran didn't understand why: he rented a tape about airtraffic controllers he saw on Discovery once, tried to tell her afterwards how he felt the same as those guys: when they finished their shift they pulled up a pew to the canteen fishtank, sat and monged out in front of the guppies and whatnot till they felt ready to go home and deal with their wife's day. All she'd said was that he was hardly an airtraffic controller and maybe he'd stop giving her colds all the time if he let her pick him up in the evening.

The streets around the station were terraces: a paperboy's dream, doors fronting straight on to the street, walk along with your sack and bang-bang-bang – no driveways, no dogs, no problem. As you walked, you could look straight in, out of the corner of your eye, bang slap into the middle of other people's quiet time. The rest of the way home you could only do it in winter, in the hour between people turning on their lights and remembering to close their curtains, but round here you could do it all year round. He smelled coal smoke, wet brick, drains, walking slowly, frowning, like his eyes were moving because he was thinking, like the last thing on his mind was seeing what people were watching.

There was no one downstairs when he got home. The TV said NO MESSAGES [PRESS MENU TO EXIT], white on blue like MS-DOS: pre-Windows, when his job hadn't existed. He called 'Hello', trying to make it sound less like a question than an admission. There wasn't any answer, so he put the kettle on, went to the foot of the stairs.

'Fran? Sweetheart?'

'Min the bath' came muffled back from upstairs. 'Joo pay the gas?'

'Yeah,' he called. 'Cuppa tea?'

'Nye get out'. Irritably.

There was a time when he could've taken the cup into her – soaped her back, whatever – while she talked about her day. But he hadn't fucked her in four months and he didn't have to see it to know that the bathroom door was closed. The kettle was starting to rumble. He went back into the kitchen, made the tea, cupped his hand under the spoon while he carried the bag to the Addis in the corner. Then he sat down at the table, started on the post.

Two for Fran, both handwritten, wonky stamps: Mount Pleasant and N4. Three for him, printed, C-thru windows showing mailmerge type, return addresses on the back to

Southend, Guildford and Leeds. When he'd split up with Charlie and got his transfer, he couldn't get arrested by a bank. Two years down the line, new mortgage, new PEP, new wife, and they were practically buzzing his house with helicopters. 7.9% till August! £250 cheque back! As a valued customer . . .

Fran came down, hair up in a turban, body wrapped in the pink fuzzy bathrobe and matching slippers he'd got her last Christmas after she'd said absolutely no more underwear this year. She went to the kettle without looking at him, so he said 'You smell nice' to her back.

'You don't,' she said, pouring the kettle on to the bag he'd left in her Far Side cup.

He sniffed theatrically at his armpits as she pulled the belt of the robe tight, dropped the bag in the sink and turned to look at him, cradling the cup in both hands.

'I smell like a man,' he said, Captain Caveman voice.

She didn't crack a smile. 'Lori's back tonight,' she said, looking at him over the rim of her cup.

He frowned. 'She alright?'

Fran hitched her shoulders. 'She broke up with that fella.'

'The black guy?'

'He was Nigerian.'

'Right.' The guy'd said his name was Echo, the one time he'd met him – he'd thought it was either a street name, or it was some art-college joke he didn't understand. You ask someone a question, they come back saying Echo. Some student thing. But Ekow, it must've been. He'd only seen it written down before, had thought it was pronounced like the green binbags at Sainsbury's.

'I'll pop round Londis, get some more Persil,' he said, trying to show he was a parent here too. When Lori was here he felt like a lodger in their family, and he'd wanted that to change for a long while.

'She's upset actually,' Fran said. That 'actually' sounded like 'back off', but probably just meant her Sloggis were up her arse about something.

'When's she get in? I could go and pick her up.'

'I think she's making her own way.'

'No trouble,' he began.

'She's making her own way,' Fran said, like that settled it, put the cup down and shuffled out into the lounge. Twenty seconds later he heard her hairdryer start, and that was it, couldn't get a word in if he'd wanted to.

Didn't get the chance later, either. Lori's connection from town got in at eight-fifteen, crafty little cow: too late for tea at home, just in time for her mum to treat her to a Harvester. Feeding up disguised as girl talk: Fran was a good mother – a good woman – and he tried to remember that. He cooked up a Sizzle and Stir with a microwave nan, took it to the sofa, forked it off his lap with the TV on. They'd both been through the let's-make-an-effort-to-eat-like-a-family in their first marriages and sometimes – most of the time – talking was the last thing you needed. When you had his job you wanted to leave it in the locker room, not come home and run through it all again. Even before the pictures.

And after them, as soon as she found out about them, all she wanted was him off the job. He told her that'd mean uniform, and did she know what uniform was like after all the balls-ups in the papers? Pensioners to puberty-dodgers calling you racialist, couldn't do your job without everyone getting their oar in.

But that wasn't where this was coming from: this was coming from they hadn't fucked in four months, and if her first husband hadn't been such a tosspot they wouldn't have a problem. Him and Charlie, his first, had worked through the three-times-a-day to the once-a-fortnight-if-you're-lucky, then sat down and agreed that if one of them felt like it they should just say it, and the other should accept that they'd both feel better afterwards, even if a Typhoo and Trio was more in the way of what they fancied. That was what you did when you were married. Fran's problem was she'd got fucked too much along the way, one-nighters no repeaters, expected to be chatted up, fawned over, flattered like men in clubs do when they're after a swift bunk-up. Marriage was supposed to be different from that, wasn't it? Not for her it wasn't; and instead of talking about it she blamed it on his job.

He wiped the plate with the nan, watched a nature show about a skeleton in Africa, a twelve-year-old boy dead of a gum abcess way back when. Kept showing him howling in the bushes to cover up the lack of facts – he was supposed to be the missing link or something, the first one they'd found with a skull big enough to worry about a mortgage. Homo Erectus. He went upstairs for an empty-house wank after, but couldn't get the hippy egghead from the show out of his mind; turning over the dead boy's vertebra in his fingers, showing the opening for the spinal cord: *the aperture is wider – see? – than that which you or I have*. The boffin said the Neanderthals thought with their spines as well as their brains. That made him feel weird, wondering if the spine in his back was thinking, if it had memories he wasn't aware of. His cock seemed to: its mind was elsewhere tonight, like so often lately. He tried the usual – armpits of Fran's dirty workshirts, face in her pillow, business end of her vibrator – but no cigar.

He put his trousers back on, found a raw silk shirt from

an Orlando factory outlet year before last, let it hang down over his strides, Florida-style. Twenty bucks – he never forgot what he paid for clothes – and made you feel like a million: the sensation against his shoulders made him long for warm air and he was hooking the ladder down from the loft before he remembered *ER*: screw it. Wasn't the same since Clooney left anyway. He took the steps gingerly, ridged aluminium cutting into his bare feet, but he took the weight on his arms till he was out on the nailed chipboard and heading for Fran's binbags by the cold water tank.

It was Florida up there alright, the spring's central heating thermals supplemented by the sun on the roof all week. There wasn't room to stand up straight as you got towards the tank, and he stooped low, hands dangling down by his knees. The stuff he wanted was underneath the bags, in the suitcase. He took a careful note of the position of the black bags, then eased the case out from under, doing the magician's tablecloth trick in slo-mo and not making a bad job of it. He undid the belt around it, checked his watch – still be making trips to the salad cart if he knew those two – and opened it up.

The Dolcis shoebox he passed over: letters, postcards, stuff he knew he shouldn't read. Similarly the Saxone: Lori's baby pics, family snaps from Fran's marriage to Marc, the wanker. He took them out and placed them side by side on the hardboard. Underneath was the Dudley box file, lifted from some stationery cupboard years ago and home to Fran's personal snaps ever since. He cross-legged on the floor in front of it, glanced once over his shoulder at the top of the ladder – like a kid up a treehouse with a grot mag – told himself not to be so stupid and got on with it.

The trick was to remember the order they came out of the box. He lifted off the top layer, put it flat on his left;

took out another handful, put them next to it. When they were all out, he started anti-clockwise, the pics from the bottom first: trikes, paddling pools, Southend; feeding a peacock on Canvey Island. Her frown, at five, was the same at forty-five. He loved her, wanted to put them all back in the box now and go down, get a round of Irish coffees ready for when they got back. Instead, he replaced them carefully into the bottom of the box, set his face as he picked up the next pile.

But it was still recs and Jungle Gyms, lions at Longleat, ponchos, tartan-trimmed flares. Grinning at the camera with her first blue eyeshadow and shiny pink lipstick, little bumps under the chest of her v-neck T-shirt. He'd been in his room above the pub then, wanking over Richard Allen paperbacks, lifting Number 6 from the newsagents when old Farnsworth was still groggily marking up the *Expresses* and *Mirrors*. Number 6 or Navy Cut, for the push-up pack: suave in Shoeburyness, thinking someone — some girl — would notice. He'd had his first *Knave* from Farnsworth's too; skimmed it off the return pile round the back one morning. No wanks were ever like your first ones. He still remembered the big, felt-tip 'X' on the cover to prevent resale, could still see this one girl from it, apple-tits, had a hat with a veil on. A way of looking at the camera. His cock was rearing out of his fly and sliding between the folds of the shirt before his brain — or his spine — caught up. It felt fucking marvellous.

When it was over, his temples were thumping from the heat, the cooked air, the sudden exertion. He thought he'd better sit still a moment, not get up till the blood had rushed back from its day-trip. He took the shirt off, dropped it in a smeary puddle behind him and sat, breathing slowly. He only turned over the next pile because it was there, started leafing through the pictures, feeling bad about it because he'd just come. Lots of red-eye in these, and Fran wearing make-up for real now: weddings and birthdays, back gardens, Margate, Dymchurch, Clacton, Terry bikini sets; I'M WITH STUPID through to FRANKIE SAYS and a full set under the cotton. A noise downstairs made him snap his head round, see what he was: a forty-year-old squatting over his second wife's teenage snaps, toss-rag festering on the floor behind him. He was down the ladder – shirt wadded up and thrown behind the water tank – and halfway down the stairs before he saw the pizza and ruby flyers feathered on the doormat. Some kid doing the rounds after school, whacking them through the letterbox, that was all. Did it pay better than papers? The hours were better, though you'd miss that feeling, dawn to drivetime, that the world was your own, shiny and clean, that this was your turf. He didn't know if people even had papers delivered any more. He went into the bedroom for a shirt.

They wouldn't be back for an hour at least, by the bedside clock. Stupid to jump like that, could've given himself a heart attack. Wanking on the sly put ants in your pants the moment your tackle was back in them: he bet it was the same for everyone, the kid in the toilet to the scrapheap geezer in his allotment lean-to. The guilt was like riding a bike, you never forgot it.

He went down to the kitchen, put the kettle on, found the Bushmill's and the squirty cream for the round of Irishes. The trick was to load the coffee with sugar, two or three spoons a head, or else the cream – even squirty – started to sink and you just got mush. He spooned Gold Blend into a jug, lined up the wine glasses. Everything ready, so the moment he heard the car he could get cracking, come through with a tray just as they sat down in the lounge. Everything ready, nothing to do but wait. He went back up to the loft to get the silk shirt, give it a rinse, hang it behind the boiler where – if Fran found it – she'd think it'd hung there since last summer.

He'd forgotten about the photos, still 52-card-pick-up'd on the chipboard floor; he knelt down, started gathering them up, putting them back how they were. He had to turn over the untouched piles to do it, stopped himself before he started going through the boyfriend-era again. Why was he doing this? He'd seen them all before. It made him feel bad to pry like this, and he was always off with Fran after. After four months without sex, off was what they didn't need.

Spotty herberts in hair gel and patterned jumpers: why did he need to look at them? They made him feel sick somewhere, even the first few as he turned them over. He could tell just by looking at them that they'd had horrible cocks – turkey-necks, or wonky round the bell-end – had he been looking at too many bell-ends lately? This particular train of thought had never come upon him when he'd looked at these pictures before.

Five gets you ten that was what it was. He hadn't asked for this job and it wasn't his fault he was conscientious at it: he had his pension to think about, and you never knew what was around the corner, most likely uniform again. You kept your nose clean and showed willing, so the day some Volvo who'd read too many *Guardian* specials tried to hang one on you, you had nothing to show but white space on your sheet. It was hard being married to a civilian. Say what you like – and he loved her – but they could never really understand. And as for Lori . . .

She'd have been telling Fran about her course all night. Art, she called it. What he had to look at all day every day she chose to make pictures of and called it Art. The art bit came in because she took the cocks out – spit-roast, doggy, cowgirl, crossbow, the men airbrushed out pixel by pixel, mouths and holes yawning wide but empty – called them things like *Nature Abhors a Vacuum*. Horrible things they were. Her tutors said she had real potential. Real potential for fucking her mum's marriage up, the selfish little mare. And him paying her course fees, expected to be grateful for the privilege. He stuffed the photos back in the box, any which way, shoved it all back in place, went downstairs and made the kettle boil so many times that when the car finally pulled up he had to trip the cut-out himself, slosh it still bubbling into the jug with the coffee grains.

The trick was the sugar.

September

He had a bad moment as they pulled up and saw the house, feeling like he was out of his depth here, feeling like he was flushing the last six months down the pan. He told himself not to be stupid – this was the pay-off, the watershed, he was convinced of it. Do this and get back on track. He followed the line of cars parked two hundred yards along the verges – 4x4s, Hyundais and Daewoos, the odd Jag, had to be a good sign – and pulled in at the first space, let the engine idle a moment before cutting it.

'You ready?' he said.

'Yeah,' she said, looking at the house. The tip of her tongue came out, put a fresh gloss on to the wine-dark lipstick. 'You?'

'Ready and willing,' he said, trying to keep it light. She didn't ask about the able.

There were two bouncers in DJs under the too-bright

carriage lamps, took their twenty quid and membership number, directed them to a room off the hall for their coats. They made him feel like the greeter at the swank hotel in Orlando had, the first real night of his honeymoon with Fran, welcoming him effusively back into the restaurant every time he'd stepped out for a slash. He took her shiny black mac off her shoulders, put it on top of his own on the piled-high sofabed in there, looked at her standing there in her boots, sheer tights, mini and tight top, her eyes done dark as Dusty's. The dress-code for the party was fetish, but mail-order took three weeks even with the web, and she'd drawn the line at going uptown to some perv shop. He'd offered to go himself, but she'd pointed out that he'd never yet got her size right, and in more forgiving fabrics than rubber as well. She'd said that what she had would do – they were only going to test the water, see what it was about, after all – but if he wanted to look like a deep-sea diver himself then he was welcome. He wore black slacks and a black silk shirt he'd found after a long hunt, hanging behind the boiler in the airing cupboard.

'I look alright?' she said.

'You look fantastic,' he said, trying to mean it with his eyes.

She tugged at the scoop-neck on her top. 'Yeah?'

He growled, made to paw her. She slapped his hand away playfully but when he went to kiss her she turned her head.

'My lipstick,' she said.

They sat on a window ledge in the lounge, sipping warm Red Bulls and avoiding eyeballing anyone. In front of them a bloke in accountant's glasses and a Hard Rock café T-shirt was getting tossed off to Celine Dion by a naked woman whose tits put Derek in mind of a couple of snooker balls dropped into a pair of nylon socks. They'd been there an hour and these were the most active people they'd seen: a couple in their thirties had been there at first, dressed up to the nines like a rap video, but they'd not seen them again; everyone else looked like pub landlords and nail salon proprietresses, and they all seemed to know each other, talking about their holidays. There were people wandering around down the garden but Fran hadn't wanted to go down there until they knew what the score was. The bloke in the Hard Rock shirt kept looking at Derek like he was asking him for something.

'You alright?' Derek asked Fran.

She nodded, pursing her lips and looking away as the snooker woman sank to her knees. Hard Rock groaned and jerked his hips, and Derek had to look away too. The size of the house had promised so much – he'd remembered that Christine Keeler film, men in DJs around a swimming pool – but inside it looked like it hadn't had so much as a J-cloth run over it in twenty years, fag burns making their own counter-pattern in the carpet.

'It's smoky,' Fran said, in a tone he couldn't gauge.

'Yeah,' he agreed, and gave it a second. They'd both seen the big magic-markered sign Blu-tacked to the hall wall by the stairs: ABSOLUTELY NO DRINK OR CIGGIES IN THE PLAYROOMS. NO THANKYOU MEANS NO, THANKYOU. HAVE FUN!!!!

'You want to stay?' she said.

'You want to?'

'It is a bit smoky in here,' she said.

He felt like he had in a bus shelter twenty-five years ago, telling Sarah Mitchell that it was alright, he had three in his jacket. The memory didn't seem to come from his head. 'It said no smoking upstairs,' he said.

'Did it?' she replied, turning her head towards him.

There was a blue bulb in the landing light, a Rasta propping up the wall underneath it. He grinned at Fran as she led Derek by the hand to the top of the wooden hill. They saw four white-gloss bedroom doors, two shut, two ajar. A rope hung across the landing beyond them.

'Y'alright?' the guy said.

'Do you just go in?' Fran asked.

He grinned, wide. She pushed open the first door, and led Derek in.

The only light came from a TV, playing blue and grey light over the bodies packed in there. It took Derek a moment to get his bearings, concentrating on covering Fran's back as he was: what he saw when his eyes adjusted was a master-size bedroom, three queen-sizes packed into it, three couples and an Asian girl on the beds, couples lining the walls. Everyone was wanking, or wanking someone else off; no one was talking, just moans and *yeah*s and wet sounds. Fran led him to a space against a wardrobe, stepping carefully over feet, discarded shoes and bags. He slipped into the space, put his back to the veneer, and she scooched her bum up against his groin, let him put his arms around her waist and watch over her shoulder.

The TV showed a silicone blonde in a classic cross-bow, two black guys doing the honours. No one was watching: they were watching each other, or what was being done to them. After a while he was hard against his wife's bum and felt like he ought to be doing something, so he smoothed his palms across Fran's hips, the front of her thighs; she put a hand on his, but instead of lifting it off her she pushed it under her skirt, let him feel where she'd cut the gusset of her tights out. He tried to do it surreptitiously but she pulled the front of her skirt up and he thought, what the hell, go with the flow; he was the only guy in the room with his flies done up, after all.

He was concentrating so hard on what his fingers were doing that at first he didn't notice the women either side running their hands over Fran's Wolfords. It was only when she gasped the third time in a way he'd never heard before that he looked down: she had each hand wrapped around the guy on either side, holding them there in what he called the parallel bars – a rare one, but you saw it in the artier stuff – while their women knelt before them working the heads while they ran their nails inside Fran's thighs. He kept his fingers moving, not knowing what to do, sweating hard with Fran's body pressed against him. The woman on the left looked up and smiled around the thing in her mouth. It all escalated very quickly.

He couldn't remember after how they'd got on the beds. No one was behaving like people, and you probably had to go a few times to get used to that. In the meantime it'd just been hands, everywhere, curves connecting, no one thinking or talking. His shirt was off while Fran was sucking him and a woman ran her hands over his back, said 'ooh, you're sweating', and licked it off his bare shoulder blades, ran her tongue down his spine making him buck hard and Fran squeal in protest. A guy started playing with Fran's bum while she knelt but she just sucked harder, going to town with it until she had to just clutch his thighs and gasp at what was being done to her. When he knelt down to help her with her clit he felt the guy going into her, and while he was still registering that, suddenly there was another guy filling her mouth. He stood back, not knowing what to do; he couldn't object, no one else was, and the guy getting blown by his wife was *smiling* at him, for fuck's sake. Grinning. He turned away and a woman in brown stockings and what looked like one of Charlie's trademark white Doreens, nothing else, pulled him further onto the bed. She was soft like a lilo and gasped like a puncture whenever he pushed: he fucked her next to the guys fucking his wife, listening to her lose it, unable to see her face. The bed was too soft and it took him a long time to come. The woman was about ready to spit in his eye by the time he finished: Fran was still going strong as he left the room, he wasn't sure where for.

They posted pictures from the party in the members-only section of the website later in the week. There weren't any with him in. The three with Fran – from the back, all the women were from the back so you couldn't see their faces – were from after he'd gone back downstairs. She'd enjoyed herself a lot more than he had, but that had to be a good thing. The only thing she'd said after was that she'd had her cap in so it ought to be alright, medically. Daewoos and Hyundais, he'd thought, driving back under the orange lights, Jazz FM on the stereo. The odd Jag.

He couldn't help himself, saved the pictures out of IE5 on the computer at work, built shortcuts onto the desktop so he could get to them when he wanted to. Looking at the pictures was a way of not thinking about it, or of processing the information outside of his head. That felt like the best thing to be doing.

He'd never looked at her back so much before, the curve of her spine. The party had shown him a kind of competence in her that he didn't seem to have: he'd know what to do better, now he knew the lie of the land. The location came as an e-mail Friday nights, was the way they liked to work it. He got through the week, same as everyone does.

Friday afternoon she rang. He turned away from the screen to take the call.

'I said yes to Dave and Angela for tomorrow night,' she said. 'That's alright, isn't it?'

'Tomorrow night?'

'Barbeque. They asked us August Bank Holiday, remember?'

'August.'

'I just found it in my diary. So I rang her and it's still on.'

'OK,' he said.

'Is it?' she said. He glanced at the screen, reached out, hit control-W.

'Yeah, course,' he said and changed the subject, stretching out his shoulders as he talked. His back was killing him.

Two Holes

SIMON LEWIS

Shirt-tails flapping, Bigpete runs into Skinnypete's bed-room, shakes Skinnypete awake, and demands, 'Lend me a belt. Please, lend me a belt.' Bright light filters through the Indian hanging Skinnypete uses as a curtain. He turns away from it and slurs, 'What? What are you doing? What's going on?'

'I'm sorry about waking you up, but it's important.'

Skinnypete hauls himself up to lean against the headboard, brushes hair away from his face, and squints up at Bigpete. 'What?'

'Have you got a belt? I need a belt.'

'No, I don't have a belt.' Skinnypete rubs his eyes and probes his furry mouth with his tongue.

Bigpete throws up his hands and exclaims 'How can you not have a belt?'

'My trousers fit. I have jutting hips.'

Bigpete steps back, looks down and gestures at his legs.

'These are my only pair of good trousers left and they're too big and they need a belt.' Bigpete's voice has the whiny intonation it gets when he's stressed, as if his vocal cords are tightening up.

Skinnypete looks Bigpete up and down. Bigpete's uniform – creased trousers, polished shoes, white shirt, plastic name badge – does nothing for him, and his face is puffy and has an unhealthy sheen. Blood wells from a shaving cut on his neck and a new zit shines under his flaky lower lip.

'They look alright to me. Just wear them low. Have the top of your pants showing like skaters do. Act like it's a fashion statement.'

'The fuckers are really uptight about uniform. Arseholes gave me shit last week. Remember? For wearing those Lara Croft socks. Doesn't fit with the image of the wanking arsehole shop. I'll get a demerit if I don't have a belt and my trousers are all droopy. I know it, they're watching me, they hate me and they're looking for excuses to bust me. They'll come down on me in a totally unreasonable way.'

'Just for not having a belt?'

'For not having a belt. They're fuckers, they're fascists, they're scum.' He sneezes suddenly and violently, which seems to come as much of a surprise to him as to Skinnypete. Bigpete is prone to sneezing fits in the morning – an allergy to the filth in the flat, he claims. The way he says it pisses Skinnypete off. He makes it sound like code for 'you should make more of an effort to clean the place up'.

'Have you seen my belt then?' says Bigpete, wiping mucus off his face with the sides of his hand.

'What does it look like?'

'It looks like a fucking belt.' Bigpete bends down and

wipes his hand on his sock. 'I wear it every day. The black leather one with the steel buckle and the extra holes.'

'Aaaaah,' says Skinnypete grinning, 'the extra holes.'

'Yeah yeah, the extra holes. I wear it every day of my life and suddenly it's gone. Have you seen it?'

'No. Did you have it on last night?'

'Yes. Probably. I don't know, do I? I was so pissed. I could have done something with it and now I wouldn't know.'

The previous night, Bigpete had come in from a long session at the pub at eleven thirty. While foraging for munchies, he had discovered four forgotten tins of Red Stripe at the back of the fridge, and they had drunk them together in Skinnypete's room while watching the ice hockey on Channel Five.

'Have you looked on the belt loops of the trousers you were wearing yesterday?'

'Of course I have. That's where it normally is.'

'Well, I'm sure it's somewhere really obvious like that.'

'I'll have to look again What's the time?'

Skinnypete picks his travel alarm clock off the bedside table. 'Eight forty-one.'

'No. It can't be. Is that clock right?'

'No, it's fast.'

'How fast?'

'I don't know. I set it a few minutes fast so that I'll think that's the real time when I wake up and then maybe I'll get up a few minutes earlier than I would have.'

Bigpete turns Skinnypete's TV on. It is conspicuously the most expensive object in the room, a Toshiba with Nicam digital stereo. It sits on a stack of breadcrates full of videos. Johnny Vaughan asks Andre Agassi where he goes on holiday.

Bigpete looks at the clock in the bottom corner of the screen and mutters to himself. 'Eight thirty-seven. Train goes eight fifty-eight. Have to leave for station at eight fifty-one. I have . . . I have . . . fourteen minutes. Oh my God. I have to find my belt in fourteen minutes.'

'I'm sure you'll find it in a couple of seconds if you just look for it properly, rather than running round and getting stressed and waking me up and giving me grief.' Skinnypete lies down and pulls the duvet over his head. 'You're going to get into one of your states. You always get like this when you're hungover.' In a practised gesture, he bunches up the duvet to create a tunnel through which he can see the TV. 'Every time I see this,' he says, 'they've got a different woman on. Who's she?' He addresses the unrecognised *Big Breakfast* presenter. 'You look like my old RE teacher.'

Skinnypete raises his head. Bigpete has left. He closes his eyes. He is cosy here. He strokes his lean belly, listens to the TV and drifts. They should bring that blonde one back. But she got married to the git with the hats. And they had one girl who was really good, what was her name? Northerner. Susan . . . no, Sarah . . . Sara Cox. Sara Cox. Yeah . . . Hmmmmmmmmmmm. It's warm in here. Sara Cox, Lara Croft, Sara Lara Cox Croft. Lara Cox. Sara Croft. Soft Lara Croft hard Sara Cox. Cox out for Lara. Skinnypete's hand slides downwards. Lara in the cot. Sara hard Cox. Oh Sara. Sara Cox in the loft. It's dark up here, Peter, I'm afraid, hold my hand. Hard cock for Sara. Ooh, you beautiful man. I'm from up north, you know, let me show you how we do things up there. Do up there. Up there. There. Just there. Oh yeah, there, there . . .

'You totally definitely haven't got one single belt?'

Skinnypete jerks upright and sits up, the duvet falling limp around him. He glares at Bigpete, who stands in the hallway, leaning into the room. 'I said already,' he snaps, and Bigpete retracts. He curses Bigpete's indecisiveness, always most in evidence when he is stressed. He must have left, faffed around at a loss for a while, and then, unable to come up with any new plan of action, returned to ask exactly the same question. The man would be useless in a crisis, thinks Skinnypete. Whereas, he rather thinks that he himself has the potential to rise magnificently to any occasion. Say Sara Cox was stuck on the top floor of a burning TV Centre. He sees himself paragliding in – Save me, Peter . . . No. Bigpete's stress has leaked out and irradiated the room, making further dreaminess impossible. Skinnypete sighs and scrapes his tongue against his teeth. He needs water. And caffeine and nicotine. Now Johnny Vaughan and that woman are caterwauling while dressed as fat opera singers. Skinnypete doesn't find it amusing at all. He glances at the time: eight forty-one. If he got up now, he reflects, all day he would feel good about being up so early. And he could get some serious creativity in.

Skinnypete clambers out of bed and slips on his dressing gown, tying the belt so that it secures his erection flat against his stomach. He shuffles into the kitchen and fills the kettle. In the room next door he can hear his flatmate thumping and crashing round. Bigpete has left a quarter-full bowl of Frosties on the table. Skinnypete picks it up and puts it beside the sink, making a note in his mental 'tidying up Bigpete's mess' file, whose contents are used to counter Bigpete's occasional 'I'm the only one that works so it's hardly fair that I have to do all the cleaning as well' missives. Looking out of the window at the dirty road, Skinnypete plans his day. Buy a pad. Laundrette. Ummmm . . . Ooh. A little thrill runs through him as he remembers that the World Bowls Championship is on later that afternoon. He makes a coffee, lights a fag, and goes to Bigpete's room to offer moral support.

Bigpete is crawling around under his bed, grunting with the effort.

'I think it's highly symbolic,' says Skinnypete, 'you losing that particular belt. Considering what you do with it.'

'Don't ever tell Kate about that,' Bigpete calls.

Sinnypete addresses Bigpete's protruding left leg. 'I won't. Course I won't. Why would I?'

Bigpete crawls out, flushed and panting and with a light dusting of fuzz on his cropped hair. 'I'm serious now. Please. You will not say anything to her about that. Ever. It was your stupid idea anyway.'

'Alright, alright.' Skinnypete flicks ash into an empty beer can. Bigpete vigorously brushes dust off his trousers. He looks so lost and distressed, Skinnypete feels sorry for him, and sincerely wants to help. He looks thoughtfully around the room. 'Is it behind the cupboard?'

'I've looked there twice.' Bigpete pulls his duvet off the bed and dumps it on the floor. He pats the sheets then gropes under the mattress.

Originally, Bigpete's belt had eight holes. At that point in his life he had slept with eight women. A rigorous no-mayonnaise-four-pint-maximum diet resulted in the need to create a ninth hole. Bigpete worked a previously unused blade of mysterious function off his Swiss army knife through the leather, then, that very same night, met, and had sex with, a dental hygienist called Lisa. It was Skinnypete who pointed out the eerie correspondence, and encouraged Bigpete to commemorate all future sexual adventures with a new belt hole. Now, two years later, the belt has eleven holes.

Bigpete pulls out and upends his clothes drawers, then

gets down on his knees and scrabbles in the pile of clothing. 'Nothing.'

'Is it behind the mirror?' suggests Skinnypete.

'Already looked.'

'What about in your laundry bag?'

Skinnypete sips coffee as Bigpete delves into the binbag where he keeps his dirty clothes. He thrashes about inside it, bursting the thin black material. A nylon sock flops through the hole.

'This is a punishment, this is,' says Bigpete, 'For allowing myself into being talked into that whole stupid hole thing.'

'You were into it at the time.'

'Yeah, well, some of us grow up and put that sort of childish behaviour behind us.

'What, shagging? Have you put that behind you now?'

'I mean running round all the time like a fucking hound with your tongue hanging out. Counting.'

'I don't count. You count.' Skinnypete didn't count, but both he and Bigpete knew very well that, if he did, he'd be on his second belt by now.

'Counted. I counted, past. I don't any more. Unlike some people I realise it's . . . meaningful relationships that count.'

Bigpete straightens, redfaced – presumably with effort, though Skinnypete wonders if it's not out of embarrassment for having used, in the heat of the moment, the term 'meaningful relationship'.

The last hole on the belt was for Kate, and that was almost a year ago. Bigpete had never declared, 'this is the one', and never saw her more than twice a week, so it had taken a long while before Skinnypete realised that there was a chance the belt would never again be repunctured.

'How's time'?'

Skinnypete looks behind him at the clock in the hall.

'It's eight forty-eight.'

'I've got three minutes,' Bigpete screeches and pounds the mattress. 'I have to leave the house in three minutes and I can't find my belt.' He forces his head hard into the bed and scrunches the sheet with shaking hands. His whole body tightens like a fist. 'Where is it? Why is it gone? Why?' His face darkens and he emits a high animal whine.

Skinnypete's voice is soothing. 'Come on, this isn't worth getting into one of your states about.' Bigpete is a big, amiable man, and few bar Skinnypete realise his secret fragility, expressed in the violent panics that occasionally wash over him.

Bigpete shakes and gasps. Skinnypete looks away, to give the man a moment with his pain. He finds himself studying a photo tacked to the wall, of Bigpete and Kate grinning under a big green leaf. He took the picture. He remembers the day: this summer, Kew Gardens. She has a white dress on that displays freckled but shapely shoulders, and her smile is wide. She photographs well, he decides.

'I want you to breathe,' he says in a low, level tone. 'Be quiet. Just think about your breathing. Slow. In and out. In and out.' Bigpete's hands gradually loosen the sheet. His great chest heaves and judders. 'In and out.' Bigpete sags.

'That's right. Come on, it'll be OK.'

Bigpete rises, flushed and panting. Skinnypete knows what he has to do. He steps forward, stands close, and pats Bigpete on the shoulder, twice. 'You alright mate?'

Bigpete nods his head, wipes his mouth, and swallows. His face is clear now, slack. He presses his palms to his cheeks. 'Yeah. I'm alright. I'm alright.'

SkinnyPete steps back. 'Good. Fuck them, eh? Fuckers.'

'Yeah. Fuckers. I hate the stupid job anyway.'

'Play it by ear,' says Skinnypete. 'See what happens.'

'Yeah.'

'You'd best be on your way, eh. Don't want to miss –'

'Your room!' yells Bigpete with a sudden convulsion. He drops his hands and turns. 'I took it off in your room, last night.' He drops his head and runs for the door, jogging Skinnypete's arm in his eagerness.

The cup jumps and coffee splashes to the floor. 'Mind' says Skinnypete. But Bigpete's explosive enlightenment is infectious, and he turns and quickly follows the clumping feet into his own bedroom. Bigpete paces the floor, wide-open eyes scanning quickly, a look of fierce concentration on his face. 'I loosened it a bit, all the booze making me swell, and then in the process of loosening it I forgot what I was doing exactly 'cause I was so pissed and I just carried on on automatic, and took it off. And dropped it. Here. On the floor.'

Skinnypete finds himself drawn into the thrill of the search, excited at the prospect of discovery. 'Or on the bed,' he suggests, 'you sat there for a while.' Skinnypete is sure he did not sleep with the belt, but it might have slipped off the bed and become jammed between the mattress and the wall. He puts his cup down, jumps on to the bed and thrusts his hand down the narrow gap.

'It's here, I know, we've got one minute to find it.' Bigpete drops down and crouches with his chin hovering inches above the carpet. He begins to rotate on his hands and knees.

Skinnypete finds that he can only reach a hand's depth into the gap; he hops off the bed, pulls the mattress a few inches away from the wall, scrambles over it and looks down. Sitting on the musty bedboard below is a tape, a condom wrapper, a broken cigarette, a pair of pants, a lump of hash and a belt. He grabs the belt swiftly, one hand just behind the buckle, the other near the tail, then pulls it out and holds it up at arm's length. 'I've found a belt,' he shouts.

Bigpete swivels and raises his head. As he gazes up at Skinnypete's catch his mouth opens slightly and his shoulders slacken. Skinnypete waves the belt like a football scarf. It's slim, of blue leather, with six big holes and an elegant, curved metal buckle.

'You lose a belt, I gain one. Some girl must have lost it down there. It could have been there for years.'

'Yes yes yes, oh yes,' says Bigpete as he clambers to his feet and snatches the belt away. He mumbles as he lifts his shirt-tails. 'I've got to get this on and get out of –' He freezes and stares down at his waistband. Skinnypete stares too. 'I've got it on.' Bigpete's voice is a harsh whisper. 'I've got my belt . . . on. I had it on all the time.' His tone rises to an incredulous warble. 'I actually had my belt on, on me, on, the whole time. Oh my God, I am, this is like, this is really unprecedented.' He sits down heavily on the bed.

'What are you like?' admonishes Skinnypete, shaking his head. 'What are you like?'

Bigpete fingers the new blue belt, turning it over and over. 'This is really shocking for me,' he mutters, 'I'm very . . .' He trails off. His forehead wrinkles. His grip tightens. 'I know this belt,' he says slowly. 'This is Kate's belt.'

'What? Naw, it could be anyone's. Hey, your train.'

'It's Kate's. I recognise the buckle.' Bigpete turns his big head, looks Skinnypete in the eyes, and enunciates clearly. 'Pete, why would Kate's belt be in your bed?' He is clutching the belt so hard that the stiff leather curls around. Where he is holding it the edges lightly touch.

Poet

TONY WHITE

He's writing a sonnet a day every day for a year and
dedicating all of them to his wife. He opens a new Word
document, and saves it as 'Sonnet.doc'. He uses thirty-six
point Arial hyphens and slashes to depict the sonnet in
diagrammatic form, breaking it down into syllables. At the
end of each line he notes the number of syllables and inserts
a rhyme key. When it's finished it looks like this.

-/-/-/-/-/-/-/-/ (10, a)
-/-/-/-/-/-/-/-/ (10, b)
-/-/-/-/-/-/-/-/ (10, a)
-/-/-/-/-/-/-/-/ (10, b)
-/-/-/-/-/-/-/-/-/ (11, c)
-/-/-/-/-/-/-/-/-/ (11, d)
-/-/-/-/-/-/-/-/-/ (11, c)
-/-/-/-/-/-/-/-/-/ (11, d)
-/-/-/-/-/-/-/-/ (1 0, e)
-/-/-/-/-/-/-/-/ (1 0, f)
-/-/-/-/-/-/-/-/ (1 0, e)
-/-/-/-/-/-/-/-/ (1 0, f)
-/-/-/-/-/-/-/-/ (10, g)
-/-/-/-/-/-/-/-/ (10, g)

Then he pastes it on to a new document as a watermark. Fiddly, but worth it. He'll only have to do it once, now, instead of looking it up every time. He saves it again and wonders how many he'll have to write before he knows the format off by heart. A week's worth? A fortnight? There's no doubt, he thinks, that it'll become second nature sooner or later. Like a new phone number that you use a lot but can't write down, or, more pertinent, when he learned to type and found his fingers waggling along with what he or other people said, or air-typing along to songs. Now, instead, he'll be counting the number of syllables in every conversation he has. He reads the template one more time.

He can just do 'Save As' every day. Sonnet one.doc. Sonnet two.doc. He's giving up smoking and his mistress of six months, and writing a sonnet every day instead. He hates upsetting people, but sometimes it has to be done. She knows it's coming. He can write them on the computer or in long hand. He'll keep it on the screen all day and do it in his coffee breaks. Finish it at home in the evening if he has to. He wonders what he should call them. Same as the file name? 'Sonnet One.doc'? Or just plain 'Sonnet One', and counting? No. Too depressing. Well, until he gets to about fifty. Dates? Nice, but 'Twenty-fifth of the Twelfth' would be a problem. He hates people who let it be known that they're working on Christmas Day. Painters, usually. Seen it in a couple of catalogues. That Jennifer Durrant show. Bloody piss artists. What do they want? A medal? He doesn't want to look like a loser. Proper titles? 'For Jeanette?' 'To His Wife on . . .' Deciding to play it by ear, he pulls down the file menu and clicks on 'Print', then walks around the corner and waits for it to appear. He tries to assume the manner of someone who's waiting for something important. A preliminary draft of his report, for instance.

Well, he is waiting for something bloody important, and anyway that doesn't have to be in until next week.

Sitting back at his desk with the template in front of him in hard copy, he opens up the Excel database that he worked late last night to finish. He's entered everything that he loves about Jeanette. There are 226 items in total. His heart expands as he reads them. He drags the mouse to select the fields. He moves the cursor to the formula bar and sorts them in ascending alphabetical order. Then changes his mind and does it descending. Perhaps he could just paste these into the sonnet template. He'd have to tweak them a bit if they didn't rhyme. There must be a good fifty sonnets' worth of material in the database. If not more. He could do a sonnet about each item, or combine them by subject matter. He does a search for all the fields that feature the word 'cunt', then counts the number of syllables in the first record. Eleven. Hmm. It could work. It could spill over into the next line, of course. There's no rule that says each line has to be a sentence in its own right, full stop. Not one that he knows of. He realises that he's unsure of the protocol for carrying a sentence over into the next line. If he did that, would he have to start the second line with a capital or not? It's a shame, he thinks, that the 'Search Fields' function doesn't stretch to rhyme. It'd be a doddle if it did. He could do a fortnight's worth of sonnets in about an hour. Hardly the point, but this self-imposed, rolling deadline does bring with it one or two responsibilities, and there'd be no harm in having a few in hand, just in case he had a bad day. It wouldn't do to have gaps. Not once he's started. He'd look stupid. Like the kind of man who starts something but can't finish it. She'd be disappointed. Angry, even. She'd look into his face for clues. He does a search for all the fields that feature the word 'come'. There are surprisingly few. He thinks for a second and then does it again without the 'e'. Finds six that involve 'coming'. Clicks on 'Save', closes the window, then opens it again and wonders whether he should do a 'Custom Header'.

Of course, looked at a certain way, this database could be seen to constitute a poem in its own right. Perhaps he should give her this. He wonders whether she'd be charmed or appalled to receive this much raw data, then decides that the sheer craft of a sonnet would be more effective. It's like a Welsh love spoon, he thinks. All the hours of work somehow self-evident but possessed of an easy grace. That's good. He decides that his sonnets should be possessed of an easy grace too. They should wear their labour . . . whatever. Lightly, yes. He highlights the column and goes to 'Insert', then selects 'New Column'. He clicks and watches as the fields move to the right. In the top-most box he types 'I love your'. He clicks on the box below and types 'I lo' and the software adds 've your'. Moving to the box below this, he types 'I' and Excel does the rest.

He carries on until he's finished the entire spreadsheet, enjoying the mindless repetition of the sequence of actions necessary. He saves it and has a momentary panic, realising with horror that in its present form the database is an act of archaeology. It's a museum, and it's finite. If he sticks to this for his material then the subject matter of the sonnets will comprise only things that happened before he decided to embark on this project. That's not the point, he thinks. It's not meant to be a substitute for life, this writing a sonnet every day. It's meant, rather, to enhance his day-to-day life. Their day-to-day life. To give both of them something to celebrate. He's going to have a bit more time on his hands, after all. Won't be working late quite as often.

He realises that he'll have to carry on adding to the

database. He can do it in the mornings just after he's logged on, when there's no one else in the office. Treat it as a small administrative task. Put it on the 'Task Bar' for a joke. He'll call the task 'D'base Maintenance', and never have to tick it, because it'll be ongoing. He can use the ten minutes between eight thirty and eight forty when he'd usually be setting up the coffee machine. The others won't mind. As long as the coffee's ready by nine, when they all come in. That's it, he thinks. This way, something which happened only yesterday, or last night, can be incorporated into today's sonnet. Something that happened that morning. There's nothing wrong with being topical. It might be tricky if they'd argued. He'd have to tread sensitively there. He wouldn't use the sonnets to settle old scores, obviously, God forbid, and it'd be no good dragging up petty stuff that would piss her off. Not that they should be too gooey. There's got to be a bit of variety. Some could be bitter-sweet. No, they couldn't. Bitter-sweet is not the tone he wants to achieve with these sonnets. Absolutely not.

He swivels on his chair and adjusts the venetian blind, then turns back to his desk and clicks his 'In Box' open. Pretending to study it, he highlights an e-mail at random and looks at the first two lines in the preview box.

They'll be more than just love poems, he decides. Any sixth-former can do those. Sonnets are different. They're the most exquisite and highly crafted poem you can write. Each one should be a world in fourteen lines. No, a universe. They're economical, he thinks, and yet, if he plays it right, each line will reveal a whole new aspect of his love for her. Even Shakespeare didn't write this many. The *TLS* will be bound to take them. Or the *Independent*. Yes. The *Independent* does poetry every day. Not that he's exactly a name in the poetry world. Would it matter, he wonders, that he's not a name in the poetry world? He isn't yet, anyway. Not really a name in any world.

He looks around the office. He can hear Steven talking in a low voice beyond the partition. No, he thinks, that's not strictly true. Within the team he's well known. He's celebrated, in fact, for the speed with which he can regurgitate an arsenal of facts and basic points of policy, give them a bit of new spin, refer to one or two Governmental URLs, decorate them with the odd table and e-mail the file to the print room with a circulation list. No one can touch him on that. It's a matter of pride that when a report needs to be done, it's him that gets put down in the 'action' column of the team meeting minutes. 'JM' are the most reassuring initials in the office, report-wise. They let everyone know that matters are in hand, and that something nice, fat and spiral-bound will be landing on their desks in a day or so. Something with a 'Scope' section and a series of action points at the front so they don't even have to read the whole thing, but if they do it'll all be there. Something that, when they've filed it, will leave little crumbs of A4 from the binding machine on their desks, and when they sweep them off on to their palm they'll be surprised at the amount of dust that's collected on the side of their hand.

It's a shame, he thinks, that reports aren't recognised as a literary genre. Not yet. Though they are, obviously. Each one as precision-crafted as a Barthelme short story. But reports have a limited audience. Not to mention time-scale. They offer nothing to the reader of the future no matter how good they are. And his are very good. He treats each bullet point like a haiku. Writes them in haiku form, sometimes, for a laugh. It has been known. And why not? A bit of exercise for the old grey matter. No one notices, obviously. They'll look again when his sonnets are collected by Faber and Faber. 'Look,' they'll say, digging out the old files. 'One-point-three. This action point on Compliance is actually a haiku, and we didn't even notice!' His office haikus will be collected on the back of the critical success of the sonnets. The collection will be called 'Total Quality Blues'. They'll be syndicated and become an office cult, reproduced on desk calendars and screen savers. Well, he thinks, reports can influence policy, in a broad sense, so they do have a kind of indirect, legacy-generating effect, but in themselves, no, they don't have any lasting value. His sonnets on the other hand will speak to posterity. Not that this is their primary function, but they'll last.

Perhaps he should stick to haikus. But, no. It's sonnets, he decides, not haikus, that are associated with love. Haikus are too obtuse. Too easy, even. He composes one in his head, to do with her putting her hand on his cock while he's driving. Fine, he thinks, but the way everything dissipates in the last line is no good. Those two big, indented, rhyming ten-syllable jobs at the end of a sonnet pack much more of a punch.

He wonders whether he should send his sonnets to the press on a daily basis, as well as to his wife. The literary world is probably just like the office writ large, he thinks. You have to target everything at the right people. Give them subtle reminders that you're here. Hold your fire until the right moment. Yes. So, perhaps he should wait until he's got a few under his belt. Probably best to do that. Send them in twenty at a time. Or he could send them weekly. Yes. Seven crisp and poignant sonnets landing in the Lit Eds' in-trays every Monday morning. Or perhaps just one a week. The best one. The PAs will start to recognise his handwriting after a while. They'll look out for them and try to read them without creasing the paper when they open the post. There'll be tears in the eyes of respected literary opinion-formers when they read them over coffee. They'll hash their phones so they can have five minutes' peace. They'll take them outside and read them in their fag breaks, the ones who still smoke, or take them to the loo. They'll look forward to Monday mornings again. They'll hand them to the subs with a shake of the head and a teary smile. They'll laugh to themselves in the backs of cabs when a particularly apposite phrase pops unbidden into their minds. They'll take them home to show their wives, or their husbands, and looking at their partners in a new light, they'll secretly wish that someone was writing them a sonnet every day, and wonder why they aren't. Give it a few weeks and they'll be getting in touch with him. They'll be asking if he has an agent. Telling him he really should, and they know just the person. There'll be a profile in the Sunday papers, and he'll be photographed naked on the roof of the British Library, holding a strategically placed typewriter, by that Magnum woman. He'll be asked to do the *Guardian* Questionnaire, and 'A Life in the Day Of'. 'I rise early,' he'll say, 'and after a breakfast of fruit and coffee I begin work on the day's sonnet.' He'll be asked to nominate his five favourite restaurants and they'll all be greasy spoons or cheap curry houses. Everyone will seek his opinion. He'll be asked to review local radio for the *Independent*. People will come up to him at black-tie parties, their right hands outstretched, shaking their heads in admiration. They'll bicker over who saw them first. People will pretend to have read them all. They'll discuss which one is their favourite.

He goes to the stationery cupboard to get a plastic wallet for his template, so that he can take it home. He'll start work on the Tube, he thinks. In long hand. He wonders how his colleagues will take it when they know that there's a poet in their midst. Steven will definitely take the piss, at first, but then that'll give way to a grudging admiration. He won't tell them yet, obviously. But eventually it'll get out. He fantasises about accidentally leaving an open copy of the *TLS* in the canteen, and how he'll break the news that the 'Jeremy P. Mayhew' sonnet on page fifteen isn't just something by an amusing namesake. 'Yes, it really is,' he'll say, coyly unfolding the News International cheque. Later on he'll tell them that the size of his advance means it's not worth his coming in any longer. A few months down the line they'll ask each other if they remember Jeremy in Policy? And did they see Tom Paulin raving about him on last night's *Late Review*? They'll do impressions of Tom Paulin hunched forward over the table, wringing his hands and saying, 'I found them pro-*found*-ly moving. This delicate . . . *testament* speaks to us all.' They'll all laugh at Tony Parsons' pithy, one-line analyses. Someone will have pinned the first couple of newspaper clippings about him on the board, and when John the Australian temp from Personnel takes down the holiday sheet in a year or so's time they'll still be there, and in the meantime the paper will have had a design overhaul and the clippings will look foolish and old-fashioned. Everyone will smile, choosing to forget the small acts of spite with which they greeted his announcement that he was leaving, and pretend they had lunch with him a lot and signed his card.

He'll give them to her every day. Leave them on the pillow, or the kitchen table. No, he'll post them. He sees her face in his mind's eye. The way she lifts her face slightly when he bends to kiss the side of her neck. The set of her jaw. They'll arrive when he's at work, and she'll phone him to tell him that she loves him too. They'll be the highlight of her day. She'll listen out for the postman, then pore over every line and ring him to ask what he means by such and such. She'll laugh to think that he noticed some intimate little action of hers, which was so small, but so telling. She'll ask him if she really does that, but secretly recognise herself in every line, and before hanging up she'll say, 'I've cooked something really special for tonight. Don't be late back, hun.' And when she's read them she'll tie them up with ribbons and keep them in a shoe box under the bed. Perhaps a couple of shoe boxes. On the odd night when he's working late, when he's away at some unavoidable conference or team-building away-day, she'll go to bed early with a camomile tea, reach under the bed for the box and read them softly to herself. She'll probably cry a little bit and miss him. Then she'll choose one of the dirtier ones and touch herself while she's reading it. The more sexually explicit sonnets will make her hot and wet. The truth of them will make her gasp. They'll cut her to the quick. She'll think about them while she's shopping, or having lunch with a friend, and be surprised by how horny they make her feel. She'll make her excuses and cut the lunch short, then rush home for a daytime wank. Or she'll phone him at work from the hotel opposite. 'Bugger your deadline,' she'll say, 'just get your ass over here p.d.q., sweetie.'

If she's having coffee with a girlfriend in town she might come across one in the paper when she's not expecting to. Her heart will swell with pride and love when she realises that the whole world is reading about her, and that they all know how much her husband loves her. Her friend will say, 'Are you OK?' but she'll just nod dreamily and say nothing. She'll check the circulation figures on the paper to see how many people know the intimate details of her private life. She'll get a kick out of that, he thinks. She'll look at people on the Tube and wonder if they've read them, and be dying to say, 'That's me! I'm his wife! He writes them for me!'

He decides not to use flowery or archaic language. He decides rather to use the language of the common man. Words like 'forsake' and 'hither' will not have a place in these sonnets. They'll be direct and to the point. Some of them will be earthy in their sexuality. Their very parochialness will make them universal. They'll be able to put this hospital thing behind them. He's glad he found her in time. Saved her life, really. She'll have to take him back.

The Puritans

TOBY LITT

Their bungalow was called Sea-View Cottage. It was located on the Suffolk coast, about seven miles south of Southwold. The walls of the bungalow were whitewash white. Had it not been for the seagull shit, the slate roof would have appeared almost perfectly black. They had moved into the bungalow in November. It was now almost April. A small lawn was dying slowly on either side of the crazy-paved garden path. Through the bay windows one could gaze directly out over the Channel, towards the Netherlands. Depending on whether the tide was in or out, the garden gate was anything from twenty to forty steps away from the water's edge. This is where Jill stood, enjoying the final ten minutes or so before she had to go back on shift.

Jill was wearing a navy blue coat over a Breton jumper, blue jeans and army surplus boots. Although there had been no discussion, the three of them had adopted this as something of a uniform. At first, John had thought wearing these kind of clothes might help them blend in with the locals. Now, they realised that their uniform merely made them stick out – but only in the way that non-locals trying to fit in anywhere always stick out. And that was a good enough reason for continuing to dress this way.

Jill had become proprietorial about the beach. Apart from the Dog-Walking Man, and the odd midwinter angler, she'd always been able to be alone here. These walks Jill called her Wind-Baths, after something Jack once said. (The proper name was Air-Baths.) Every morning for the past five months Jill had made an enjoyable little ritual of them – walking, in as straight a line as possible, from the bungalow to the sea. On the way, she collected pebbles, driftwood, rope, plastic. Anything that she could reach without having to step off her imaginary straight line. The beach was empty, open. The beach helped her to clarify herself.

This morning the world felt delightfully mellow. The breeze wasn't exactly warm, but the terrifying North Sea chill was for the first time this year entirely absent.

Jill turned to look back at the bungalow. The sight of it still gave her pleasure. Sea-View Cottage was perfect for their purposes. On the outside, it looked like any other bungalow. But the man who built it, back in 1979, had been taking the Cold War very seriously. Embedded six feet beneath the foundations of the cottage was a nuclear fall-out shelter of similar dimensions to the upstairs rooms. It was entered through a pair of metal doors, and down a flight concrete stairs.

Two other white and black bungalows stood to the left and right of Sea-View Cottage: Kittywake (after a kind of seagull) and The Old Cove (after someone with a shit sense of humour). Since November, both had remained empty and unvisited.

Jill started back towards their bungalow. She hadn't gathered anything much this morning, only a piece of driftwood of a particularly exquisite grey. She intended to nail this to the living-room wall, as part of her collection of particularly exquisite grey pieces of driftwood.

Back in London, Jill had been a website designer. She liked to think that what she once did with Dreamweaver 2.0, she now did with real, physical objects. Only she did it a lot better. And it was a great deal more satisfying.

Halfway back to the bungalow, she spotted a floppy circle stuck on top of a grey rock. These rings were all the sea left of condoms, before it shredded them completely. Jill peeled the circle off the rock and stuffed it in her side pocket. She had a nailed-up collection of condom rings, too.

Just then, she heard a car engine. It was getting louder. She hurried towards the cottage. By the time she reached the garden gate, the car was negotiating the last couple of hedge-hidden bends in the muddy lane.

Jill knew that whoever it was, it wouldn't be anyone they knew. When they had left London, she and Jack hadn't exactly advertised where they were going. Or what they'd be doing when they got there. Steve, and Steve alone, knew their location. (Steve was their boss.)

She hid herself in the porch, listening. The car drew up outside Kittywake.

Jill crouched down. A car door opened. The engine kept running. The gate squeaked. The car moved forwards. The engine was cut off. The gate squeaked shut. Another car door opened.

'Well, we're here,' said a male voice.

'Yes, we're here,' replied a female voice.

They sounded young.

'This is going to be fun,' said the man.

'Fun-fun-fun,' said the woman.

Jill listened a moment more, as the young couple opened the boot and began to unload. Then she slipped inside as quickly and quietly as possible. She now had two minutes until she was due on shift. She would tell John about the newcomers when she went down into the basement. He could then pass the information on, when Jack woke up.

Just to make double-sure, she wrote a message on the white board in the kitchen. *A couple have arrived at Kittywake. Caution. Meeting tomorrow morning?*

She looked over the food on the square, white-painted table. Since moving out of London, she had learned to bake bread. It was something she'd always wanted to do. The loaf on the table, ready for John to toast, was one she had made yesterday. The milk, butter and eggs came from a farm down the road. Even the marmalade, bought from a church sale, was homemade. Only the teabags seemed in any way industrial. She would get the household on to loose-leaf soon.

'Jill!' John shouted up from the basement.

She knew she should always be a little early for the handover. Otherwise John got angry. It was just the light had been so beautiful outside. And then she'd been delayed by the newcomers.

The car boot slamming only ten yards away made her jump. She was no longer used to such loud, unexpected noises.

'Jill!' John called, louder.

Jill laced her fingers together and pushed them away from her until they clicked. Then she went downstairs into the basement.

*

The system was this: they each worked one of three eight-hour shifts: morning (7 a.m. to 3 p.m.) evening (3 p.m. to 11 p.m.) night (11 p.m. to 7 a.m.) The machines they used were AMX-3000s. As videos, unlike audio cassettes, can't be high-speed copied, all the tape-to-taping had to be done in real time. It therefore took an AMX-3000 60 minutes to make a decent enough second generation of a 60-minute master. With 20 machines running in tandem, they were turning out 20 videos an hour; 480 a day; 13,340 a month. It was important they kept the machines going twenty-four hours a day. Steve had customers waiting. Customers it wasn't a good idea to disappoint. Steve collected the completed tapes a couple of times a month. He wasn't pleased if they hadn't gone through all the boxes. And so, they stuck religiously to their shifts. At the moment, Jill was on mornings, Jack on evenings and John on nights. In seven day's time, when the month came to an end, they would all have two whole days off. When they started up again, Jill would be on evenings, Jack on nights, John mornings.

For this, they were well paid. They all cleared several thousand a month. Avoided tax. And had hardly any outgoings. The money, paid to them by Steve, in cash, just seemed to stack up. In drawers. Under mattresses. None of them dared use a bank. Six months in, and already they didn't know what to do with it all.

The video they were doing at the moment was an ultra-violent Swedish hardcore flick. It was mostly gay sex, although a woman made a brief but memorable appearance. The images weren't the kind of thing any of them were likely to get off on. (Although Jill sometimes had her doubts about John.) At the start, she had tended to watch each video through – just to see what it was about. They soon became very monotonous. Blood was involved. And screaming. And shit. Lots of shit. She still fast-forwarded through the new tapes — making sure there weren't any children involved. That had been her only stipulation when she took the job.

Despite the equality of the shift-system, Jill tried to stay away from John as much as possible. She'd disliked him from the moment they'd met. She thought him seedy. He kept his past infuriatingly — Jill thought *deliberately* infuriatingly — mysterious. From what Jack and Jill had been able to gather, it involved drugs, in quantities vaster (John hinted) than any they had ever come across. And prison, also. For the time being, though, John said all he wanted to do was 'mellow on back to grass-roots'. If this meant smoking dope, they'd soon learned it did anything but make him mellow.

Because Jill and Jack were coupled up, they tried to maximise their shared off-time. She only got out of bed an hour before her shift began; he went to sleep as soon as his finished. This left them from about 6 p.m. to 11 p.m. to hang out.

The three of them were only ever together when a meeting had been called. Usually, only John called meetings. And then, it was usually to complain about something (the food, usually). But the arrival of the newcomers was something they *had* to talk about. It was very unusual. Which is why Jill had called the meeting.

Jill got up at 5 a.m. especially. Jack was still awake, eight and a half hours after his evening shift had finished. John, coming to the end of the night shift, was waiting for them when they descended the stairs into the basement. As the three of them talked, he kept working — taking tapes out of cardboard boxes, putting them in machines, copying, checking, taking tapes out of machines, putting them in cardboard boxes. The machines made a loud, slightly grindy whirring sound.

'I think one of us should go round,' said Jill, having to raise her voice a little. 'You know, to say hello. We need to appear as normal as possible, don't we?'

'Why?' said John. 'None of us are. And I bet they're not either.'

'You know exactly what I mean,' said Jill.

'Hey,' Jack said, 'let's think about this.'

'We should never let them in the house,' said John. 'We can be perfectly polite and all that. But they must never come inside.'

'Won't that make them suspicious?' said Jill.

'Of what?' shouted John. 'If they come in, even only into the kitchen, they'll hear that something's going on down here.'

He patted one of the machines. It continued to whirr.

'We could tell them it's the boiler,' said Jill.

Most of the time, Jack kept quiet. He knew that his attempts to peacemake only inflamed the others. John accused him of being in Jill's pocket. Jill tried to force him to agree with her. Generally, he did agree with Jill. But, because of that, he worried that John was right, and that he *was* in Jill's pocket. 'Why don't we leave it,' he suggested, 'and just see what happens?'

'No,' said Jill. 'We need a policy.'

'I agree,' said John, making one of his unexpected tactical switches. With only three of them, realignments like this were always decisive. They operated democratically, and two was an instant majority.

'OK,' said Jack.

'I think Jill should go over and make friends with them,'

said John. 'They're less likely to suspect a woman.'

'Oh, thanks,' said Jill.

'Of doing what we're doing,' John said. They both looked at Jack.

'Well?' said Jill.

'Fine,' he said, still surprised they were agreeing.

'Fine,' said John. 'Then I'm going to bed.'

As soon as he was out of earshot, Jill said, 'Do you think he means it?'

That afternoon, a couple of hours after coming off shift, Jill went round and knocked on Kittywake's front door.

When she'd introduced herself, the young woman invited Jill in for tea.

The kitchen was very warm, overheated by an Aga. A couple of cardboard boxes full of food were jammed against the far wall.

'I'm Molly,' she said. 'And this is – '

'Mark,' said the good-looking young man, getting up from the bleached pine table.

They were both around twenty-two, twenty-three. Five or six years younger than Jill and Jack, and eight less than John.

'We're just here for a week,' said Molly, after they'd sat down around the table. 'Getting out of London.'

'What are you doing here?' asked Mark.

'I live here,' said Jill. 'For the moment, at least.'

'But you're not *from* here,' said Molly.

'Not originally, no,' Jill replied. 'I'm living here with my boyfriend –' She decided at that moment not to mention John. He would just have to keep out of sight for a while.

'What do you do?' asked Mark.

Jill had to think about this. 'I'm an artist,' she said.

'Oh, really,' said Molly. 'What kind of thing?'

'I work on the beach, mostly. I collect things and put them together. It's not very original or anything. I just do it for myself, you see.' Jill realised she was gabbling, but she couldn't stop herself. Here, at least, was something she could be honest about. 'It's good therapy.'

'I'd love to see some of your stuff,' said Molly. 'Me, too,' said Mark.

'I don't really show anyone,' said Jill.

'Not even your boyfriend?' asked Mark.

'No, not really.'

By the time she got back to Sea-View Cottage, Jill had found out all about Molly and Mark. She knew they both worked in the theatre, but only backstage. That they both – just like Jack – wanted to break into film. That Molly was two months pregnant, and that the two of them were trying to fit in as many little holidays as they could before the baby was born.

'I just wanted some fresh air,' said Molly.

'We got the address off some friends who came last year,' added Mark.

'Isn't it lovely?' said Molly.

Jill went down into the basement, where Jack and John were awaiting her.

'Well, they *seem* harmless enough,' she said.

When the meeting was over, Jack and Jill went upstairs to their bedroom. They got in under the covers for a clothes-on cuddle. All of a sudden, they both started giggling.

'I can't believe you forgot to tell them about John,' said Jack. Jill giggled some more.

'Well, you know,' she said, 'I probably subconsciously

wanted to punish him for being so horrible to us all the time.'

Jack said, 'So now, he'll have to stay hidden 'till they leave.'

'Good,' said Jill.

They rubbed noses, like they always did.

'So, you're not worried about them,' said Jack.

'As long as they don't find out what we're doing,' said Jill, 'We'll be fine.'

As Jill was Wind-Bathing and beachcombing the next morning, Molly trotted up alongside her.

'Mind if I join you?' she said.

'No,' said Jill. She found it slightly disconcerting to know this young woman was pregnant, but not be able to see it.

'This beach is so lovely,' said Molly. 'So desolate.'

'I find it quite cosy,' said Jill.

'Cosy, too,' said Molly.

Jill felt all the advantages of being a twenty-seven-year-old talking to a twenty-two-year-old.

They walked to the water's edge.

'It just makes me feel so clean and refreshed,' said Molly, and stuck her arms out to either side.

As she stood there with her eyes closed, Jill took the chance to look Molly over. Molly's hair was reddish, and her skin fashionably freckled. At least, that had been the latest trend in models the month. Jill left London. However, there was an unlovely clenchedness about Molly's face. It was too hard. Vertical lines were incised on either side of her mouth. Jill knew them for what they were: speed-cuts.

'Whoo,' said Molly, when a stronger than usual gust of wind almost made her take a step backwards.

She opened her eyes before Jill had a chance to look away.

'It's not Mark's baby,' said Molly. Then added hurriedly, 'I don't know why I told you that.'

Jill was stunned. 'Does he know?' she said.

'No,' said Molly, 'I brought him here to tell him.'

That evening, there was a knock at the door of Sea-View Cottage. As agreed, Jill answered. It was Mark. She was very aware of the whirring sound of the tape-to-tape machines.

'We were wondering if you'd like to come round to dinner,' said Mark. 'Not tonight. Tomorrow. Both of you.'

'That would be very nice,' said Jill, images of blood and shit flashing behind her eyes. 'I don't think we could stay very late.'

'No problem,' said Mark. 'How about six?'

'Jack doesn't like to stay out too late,' said Jill.

'See you at six, then.'

Jill closed the door, keeping the whirring sound in.

The next morning, Molly again joined Jill on the beach.

'Did you tell him yet?' asked Jill.

'What?' said Molly. 'About the baby?'

'Yes,' said Jill.

Molly looked thoughtful. 'No,' she said. 'It's just too difficult. You didn't tell Jack, did you?'

'Of course not.'

'I'm *so* looking forward to meeting him. I don't want him to feel at all awkward. At dinner.'

'I didn't tell him anything.'

Molly started the conversation again. 'You and Jack eat everything, don't you? I'm going shopping today. I don't want to get anything *wrong.*'

'Oh, there's *nothing* we won't eat,' said Jill.

They both laughed.

Jack and Jill knocked on the door of Kittywake at ten past six. Jack held the bottle of red wine.

It was Mark who answered. 'I'm afraid Molly isn't feeling very well,' he said, and mimed puking. 'Sorry I couldn't come round and tell you earlier. I didn't want to leave her alone.'

'We understand,' said Jill. 'Shall I go in and see her?'

'I think she'd prefer it if you didn't see her this way.'

'Hope she gets better soon,' said Jack.

'How about we do it tomorrow evening instead,' suggested Mark.

'Lovely,' said Jill.

Molly did not join Jill on the beach the next morning. The air was wet with sea-spray. A solitary seagull walked along behind her.

Jill's first thought was that Molly was still feeling sick. But then she realised that she might, at that very moment, be telling Mark the truth about the baby. The morning seemed an odd time to do it, but you never knew with other people. If she did tell him, he'd almost certainly get into a real state. It wouldn't surprise her at all if he got into the car and drove off.

She looked back towards Kittywake, but it gave little sign as to what was going on inside. Tufts of white smoke were ripped away from the chimney-stack as soon as they appeared.

That evening, they turned up on Kittywake's doorstep again: Jack with the same bottle of wine; Jill with some wild flowers she had gathered for Molly.

It was Molly who answered the door. 'Oh, come in,' she said.

'Feeling better?' asked Jill.

'Much,' said Molly. 'You must be Jack.'

The smell of butter-frying garlic suffused the hall. They walked through into the kitchen.

'Hi,' said Mark, and wiped his hand on a dishcloth before holding it out towards Jack. He was halfway through slicing a chopping-board full of kidneys.

'Mark,' said Jack.

'Jack,' said Mark.

'Sit down,' said Molly.

They began to talk, mostly about the film industry. The conversation was good, if a little awkward at times. Molly was charming. Mark was amusing, in a slightly sarcastic way. He seemed to enjoy gently torturing Molly.

The food, when it came, was delicious. Stilton soup. Kidneys on a bed of rocket with garlic mash. Even the plastic tubs of gooseberry fool tasted almost homemade.

'It's terrible,' said Molly, as they were having coffee. 'We're only here another three days. The time seems to have gone by so fast.'

Jill looked at her. She was obviously referring to not having told Mark.

'I want to show you something,' said Molly suddenly. She grabbed Jill by the hand, tugged her into the bedroom and slammed the door behind them.

Jack and Mark were left alone in the kitchen.

Mark wasted no time in leaning over to Jack. 'Molly isn't pregnant, you know,' he said. 'She lost the baby about five months ago. Just before Christmas. It sent her a little bit mad.'

'Really?' said Jack.

'I just play along with it, most of the time. It's better than having her constantly in hysterics.'

Jack thought this an odd comment. 'What do the doctors say?' he asked.

'She's in denial, plain and simple. She's been two months pregnant ever since November.'

'That must be difficult for you,' said Jack.

'I can cope,' said Mark. 'But please don't tell Jill. It's better if there's at least one person who can be completely natural with her.'

'I understand,' said Jack, thoroughly confused.

Just then, Jill came out of the bedroom. In her hands she held a half-knitted baby sweater. 'Isn't it cute?' she' said.

Jack was half an hour late in relieving John that night. He and Jill hadn't said anything much on the short walk home.

'Nice people.'

'Yes,' replied Jill.

'Strange.'

'Very strange.'

John was pretty pissed off at having to stay hidden the whole time. 'Don't tell me how nicey-nice it was,' he said, before stamping upstairs. 'Because I don't want to fucking know.'

Jack knew what John would do now. Head straight for his Technics decks in the living room, put on his massive headphones, close his eyes and pretend he was DJing at some superclub in Ibiza.

During the night shift, Jack decided he'd better not tell Jill that Molly was mad. He'd wait until after Mark and Molly had gone back to London.

The next morning, the beach was aslant with rain. It was colder, too. Determined never to miss a day, Jill put on her waterproofs and went out to take her Wind-Bath. The weather being what it was, she hardly expected to see Molly outside. And so, when she heard Kittywake's front door slam shut, Jill was a little startled. But, on turning round, she saw that it was Mark and not Molly who was walking towards her.

'Morning,' he hollered, when he'd caught up. 'What are you doing out in this?'

'I don't mind it,' yelled Jill. 'How's Molly?'

'Not too bright today, either.'

'Oh dear.'

They walked towards the sea.

'You know,' Mark shouted conversationally, 'Molly and I haven't had sex since she got pregnant. Not once.'

'Oh,' said Jill.

'She just . . . doesn't want to. Says the very thought makes her feel ill.'

'Perhaps that's understandable. A lot of women feel that way.'

'Yes, but what am I meant to do?' he asked. 'Never have sex again?'

'I'm sure she'll come back to the idea.'

'I'll have exploded with frustration by then. I need to have sex regularly. It's like breathing or something.'

Jill stopped. 'Why exactly are you telling me this?'

'Why do you think?'

'I hope it's not what I think it is.'

'What *do* you think it is?'

'I'm going back inside.'

'What do you think I meant?' Mark stood in her way. *'What* do you *think* I *meant?'*

Jill tried to wither him. 'How can you be so crass?'

Mark leaned closer, so he didn't have to shout. 'It's the touching I miss, as much as anything. She never even does that any more.' Mark was sticking his hands down the front of his trousers.

Jill dodged to one side, then back the other way. Mark, a little off-balance to begin with, was wrong-footed.

She sprinted up the beach. As she neared Sea-View Cottage, she saw Molly standing on the porch in her dressing gown. Molly waved and smiled.

Jill spent most of her shift feeling furious with Mark. But when she calmed down, she began to feel sorry for Molly. If she told Molly about Mark, she might leave him. And if that happened, the baby would lose its father. Who was she to risk making that happen?

She really wanted to tell Jack. But Molly had looked so vulnerable, standing on the doorstep. Jill decided she'd tell Jack all about it, after Molly and Mark had left.

In the afternoon, when they were in bed together, Jack asked Jill what she thought of Molly.

'She's very nice,' said Jill. 'Why do you ask?'

'I don't know,' said Jack. 'She's just a bit young to be pregnant, isn't she?'

'Perhaps it was an accident.'

'Perhaps.'

They were silent for a while.

'What do you think of Mark?' Jill asked.

'I'm not sure I like him very much.'

'Why not?'

'He seems a bit creepy.'

Jill felt very relieved. 'I agree,' she said. 'There's something indefinably nasty about him.'

'Do you think they'll think it's odd, us not inviting them back for dinner?'

'Let them think whatever,' said Jill. 'They'll be gone in a couple of days.'

About two in the morning, just as he'd finished changing over another twenty tapes, Jack thought he heard someone knocking on the front door – knocking hard. But John was upstairs. If it *was* the door, then he'd get it. The knocking came again. John was at his decks in the living room, taking his imaginary Ibiza to a higher level.

After closing up the basement, Jack went to investigate. Molly was there, wearing only a dressing gown. She didn't look at all pregnant. 'Can I come in?' she said.

Jack didn't seem to have a choice. John was in the living room. Jack led Molly through into the kitchen. 'Noisy, isn't it?' he said, meaning the whirring sound.

'Don't worry,' said Molly. 'I won't stay long.'

'It's the boiler.'

Jack sat down, terrified that at any moment John would come through to fetch another beer from the fridge.

'Are you alright?' asked Jack.

'I'm fine. I'm fine. I just had to come and tell you,' she hesitated. 'This morning, on the beach. I think something happened between Mark and Jill.'

'Something, what?'

'Well, it's pretty obvious that they're attracted to each other, isn't it?'

Jack thought about this for a moment.

'I saw them *kissing,*' said Molly.

'No,' said Jack.

'I did,' Molly said. 'He thought I was still asleep, but I looked out the window and saw them.'

'I don't believe you,' said Jack. He felt quite convinced

that this delusion was another sign of Molly's madness – as well as believing herself pregnant, she had started to believe her boyfriend was shagging other women.

'But it's true,' said Molly, a little too loud for comfort. Even with his headphones on John might hear. The records he played did, now and again, have quiet bits.

'I think we should get you back to bed.'

'Why don't you believe me?'

'I do,' said Jack. 'I'm just sure it didn't mean anything. Come along.' He put his arm around Molly and led her to the front door. While they'd been talking, the whirring sound of the machines had ceased. Luckily, Molly didn't seem to have noticed. Her torch was on the doorstep, lit but pointing into the concrete.

'I'll come with you,' Jack said.

They walked down Sea-View's garden path, through the gate, along a dozen yards to the right, through Kittywake's gate, up the path.

Before they'd even reached the door, Mark had yanked it open. 'What's all this, then?' he said.

'Molly just . . .' but Jack didn't know what to say.

Molly elaborated the lie for him, 'I wanted to talk to Jill about something.'

'Yes,' said Jack. 'And I was just walking her back. Quite innocent.' Molly turned as she went in the door. 'Thank you, Jack,' she said. 'And say thank you *so* much to Jill, too.'

'I will,' said Jack.

By the time he'd got back to the machines, Jack reckoned he'd lost about twenty minutes.

The tapes which had been building up for a fortnight were due to be collected the following night. The routine was this: Steve, accompanied by either Geoff or Keith, arrived around midnight in the van. They took two and half hours in total to unload the blank tapes and then load up the finished ones. They were usually well away before it started to get light.

Jack felt anxious about collection day all through his shift. He already knew he couldn't mention anything about Molly's midnight visit to Jill. He was sure that Molly had been lying, though she might not know it herself.

During the night, Jack had started copying a new movie. He watched it through at normal speed on their quality control machine. It was the hardest porn he had ever seen: camcordered in a concrete bunker of some sort, five ugly men raped an ugly woman, and then each other. He could see the woman trying to fight back, even though she was obviously smacked off her tits. The violence was homicidal.

He wanted to tell Jill not to watch it, but he knew that – if he did – she would slam it on the moment he left the room.

The shift passed very slowly. When Jill came to relieve him, he gave her a big kiss. She looked at his box of uncompleted tapes.

'I dozed off,' he said, before she asked.

During her sleepless night, Jill had almost decided to tell Jack about Mark's clumsy pass the previous morning. For the first time since they arrived, she'd not gone out for her Wind-Bath. She hadn't wanted to risk meeting Mark alone again. In some ways, he'd ruined the beach for her.

Jack went to bed. But he couldn't sleep. After half an hour, he went back down to see Jill. She was watching the new movie, and was obviously quite sickened. 'I have to tell you something,' he said. 'You have to promise to keep it a secret.'

'Yes?' asked Jill, putting the tape on pause. 'What?'

'Promise.'

'I did.'

'Molly isn't pregnant,' Jack said. 'She just thinks she is because she lost another baby.'

'Rubbish,' said Jill.

'Mark told me the other night, when we were round at dinner. You were in the bedroom. Looking at baby clothes. Molly's a bit mental.'

'She's not.'

'Well, you don't have to believe it. I just wanted to tell you, so you knew.'

Jill thought for a moment about returning the favour, and telling Jack about Mark not knowing the baby wasn't his. But if there wasn't a baby, or even if Jack just believed there wasn't, then that didn't really mean anything.

'You're nuts,' she said, and kissed him. 'Go back to bed.'

That evening, Molly appeared on the doorstep. Jill answered when she knocked.

'Hello,' said Molly, a little formally.

'Hi.'

'We wondered if you'd like to come round to dinner again. Tonight's our last night. I know it's a bit short notice. We'd like to see you both again before we go.'

'Oh,' said Jill. 'Lovely.'

Molly beckoned Jill to come outside. They went a few steps down the garden path. 'I told him,' said Molly.

'My God,' said Jill. 'How was he?'

'Much better than I thought it would be.'

Jill didn't know what she believed any more.

'He says we can always have one together in a few years' time.'

'Does he know the father?'

Molly blushed, very convincingly. 'It's his best friend from school.'

'That's terrible,' said Jill, at that moment believing it.

'I know,' said Molly, naughtily.

'Can you come around seven?'

'We'll be there,' said Jill.

'We can't go,' said Jack when Jill told him. He was still a little worried about letting Jill and Mark spend any more time together. Even though he knew Molly was mad, he thought there had been some truth in what she'd said about the other two being attracted to each other. The fact that he himself fancied Molly seemed somehow to confirm this.

'We have to,' said Jill. 'Anyway, they'll be gone tomorrow morning. What harm can it do?'

'Steve is going to be shifting half a ton of extremely hard-core porn into the back of his van tonight,' said Jack. 'What *harm* is it going to do?'

'We'll just tell him to keep it quiet.'

'They're *bound* to notice.'

'What do you want to do? Tell me.'

'Phone him. Tell him not to come. Tell him to come tomorrow.'

'He won't do that,' said Jill.

'We'll tell him the police are sniffing around.'

'He'd just come to see for himself.'

Jack knew this was true. 'I'm going for a walk,' he said.

'You haven't got time,' said Jill.

'Do you *want* to get us caught?' shouted Jack. 'Do you know what will happen if they catch us with this stuff?' He picked up a tape and hurled it towards the bedroom wall. Frustratingly, it didn't shatter. Just landed flat and dropped to the floor.

'I'm *going* for a walk,' Jack said. 'Don't worry – I'll be back in time.'

Jack was halfway down the garden path when he spotted Molly. She was standing right in front of Sea-View Cottage, looking down the beach. There was no way he could get past without her noticing. He thought for a moment about going back into the bungalow, but he was too angry with Jill for that. He needed to walk away from her for a while. He needed to let himself think that he might, perhaps, never go back.

When she heard the latch of the garden gate being lifted, Molly turned to see who it was.

'Jack,' she said, apparently relieved.

'Molly,' said Jack. He intended to walk straight past her, and on towards the shoreline. Without being rude, of course.

'I was waiting for you,' Molly said. 'I was hoping you'd look out and see me standing here.'

'Did you?' said Jack.

She took a couple of steps towards him. 'You were so kind when I came round last night.'

'It was nothing.'

'No,' said Molly. 'No, it wasn't.'

She was now close enough to touch him, which she did. She reached out with one of her hands, and gently stroked his cheek.

He flinched away. 'Get off,' he said.

'Mark's busy cooking,' said Molly. 'We could find somewhere to go.'

'But you're pregnant,' Jack said.

Molly took another step forwards. 'You know that's a lie,' she said.

'Fucking hell,' said Jack, backing away. 'What the fuck is wrong with you?'

Molly followed him. Jack tried to twist round, so that he could run. But the sand slipped away under his feet, and he fell on his side.

Molly jumped on top of him. 'That's more like it,' she said. With her groin, she pressed down on his hips. When he reached to try and push her off, she grabbed his wrists.

'Don't,' said Jack, warning violence.

Molly was surprisingly strong. Jack struggled, but Molly was able to ride him.

'Let *go*!' he shouted.

'Only if you kiss me.' Without waiting for a response, Molly pushed her face down on his. Their teeth clicked sharply together.

'Fuck,' said Jack.

They were close up against the garden fence of Sea-View Cottage – out of sight of either porch. Molly pressed down again. He could feel her tongue licking along his lips.

He tried again to push her off, and this time he succeeded – but only because she let him.

She landed, quite hard, on her back, on the grass. As he scrambled to one side, he heard her saying, *'Beat* you.'

After a second to get his breath, Jack stood up. 'You are sick,' he said.

She closed her eyes and pretended to sunbathe. 'Would you mind,' she said, 'you're standing in my light.'

For a moment, Jack thought he wasn't going to kick Molly – then he did kick her. His toes caught her thigh. She doubled up, and he guessed he'd dead-legged her. He bent down. He was about to start apologising when he heard her whisper, 'Now that's more like it.'

Jack turned away.

*

Jack was only a few steps away from the porch when Jill opened the door. 'I'm sorry,' she said.

'Let's go inside,' he said.

'I said I'm sorry.'

'OK,' he said. 'Apology accepted. Inside.' He felt himself on the point of shoving her. She was looking dangerously out over the beach. 'We need to get ready,' he said. She took a final deep breath, and turned back through the door. Just then, Jack saw Molly standing up from behind the garden fence. He almost leapt through the door into the bungalow.

Jack and Jill took another bottle of the same red as before round to Kittywake at seven o'clock.

'Come *in*,' said Molly.

'How *are* you?' said Jill.

'Oh, very well,' said Molly, looking directly at Jack.

They walked through the hall and into the kitchen. Jack felt Molly pinching his bum.

'Hi,' said Mark, who had just been prodding something in the oven.

'Smells lovely,' said Jill.

Mark kissed her on both cheeks, and she was in control enough to let him.

'Make yourselves at home,' said Molly.

They sat down in the same places as before. Jack immediately felt Molly's toes crawling up his calf. He reached down and pushed them away. They started again, at the ankle.

'It's not quite as elaborate as last time,' Mark said. 'I'm afraid we were using up the last of our food – so it's baked bean surprise.'

'Lovely,' said Jill.

*

The meal was torture for Jack and for Jill. Molly kept pestering Jack beneath the table, both with feet and with hands. Jack tried his best to ignore her pinchings, strokings and fondlings. Mark sent yearning looks in Jill's direction. Jill tried to avoid them as best she could. Jack, even whilst being distracted by Molly, couldn't help but notice what Mark was doing. He looked at Jill, to see if she was reciprocating. Jill caught Jack looking at her a couple of times. She knew what he was thinking. To reassure him, she started directing all her conversation towards Molly. This only made Jack's under-the-table situation more desperate.

The food was fairly disgusting: undercooked potatoes on top of a mess of lukewarm baked beans and half-cold Spam.

After they'd finished eating, Molly took Mark's hand and said, 'We've decided that, if the baby's a boy, we're going to call it Jack, and if it's a girl, we'll call it Jill.'

'I don't know what to say,' said Jill. She avoided eye-contact with everyone around the table, including Jack.

'That's incredible,' said Jack, unable to stop himself sounding sarcastic.

Just then, they all heard an engine coming down the lane.

'I wonder who that is,' said Mark, getting up and going to the back window.

Molly went to join him there. 'It's a white van,' she said. 'It's coming this way. Is it some friends of yours?'

Jack looked anxiously at Jill. 'It might be,' she said.

'Well, don't you know?' asked Mark. 'You must have arranged it, if you know them.'

The van's lights raked through the candle-lit kitchen. The horn pipped three times, making everyone jump. Jack and Jill, looking at each other desperately, heard the engine switch off.

'It's a man,' said Molly.

They heard the van door open, then slam. Jack leaned over to Jill and whispered in her ear, 'What do we do?'

'He's coming this way,' said Mark.

'He looks very tough,' said Molly. 'He's wearing a long leather coat.'

Jack got up out of his chair and crossed quickly to the window. He was just in time to see Steve disappear behind the side wall of Kittywake. For a moment, everyone stood still. Then Steve walked through the hall and into the kitchen, leaving the front door banging open behind him.

'Mol,' he said, nodding. 'Mark.'

They nodded back at him.

'What?' said Jack.

'Oh,' said Steve, 'I see you lot have already met.'

'Do you *know* them?' said Jill.

Just then, John sprinted through the open front door. He came straight into the kitchen, very much as if he'd been there before. 'Molly,' he said, with a wink.

'About fucking time,' said Steve, angrily. 'You and Molly grab ahold of her. Me and Mark'll get this one here.'

Lovers

REBBECCA RAY

It was a Tuesday in April when she came home and said to her parents that she wouldn't be living there any more. She didn't say it like that, she said that they'd found a place, like the moving in was more important than the moving out, like the way they say at weddings that you're gaining a son, you're not losing a daughter. She said it like that. She said the place was perfect.

'That's wonderful,' her mother said, and she reached across to touch her hand.

'It's great,' her father said. He came over to stand next to her mother, to put his hand on the back of her neck.

She talked about all the things that they'd given her for birthdays and Christmases and how good they'd look in their new place. She tried to use words that included them – when you come and have dinner, she said, when you come and stay for a while. And they did come and hug her and they smiled at her but mostly they just stood together.

They said things at the same time and then they laughed together and were quiet.

She took them around to see the flat on Thursday. The corridor outside the flat was narrow and it had carpet, they couldn't hear their own feet when they walked. There wasn't enough room for them to stand together there, they were crowded against the walls. There weren't any windows in the corridor either. Her mother saw this, looking around, holding her bag in both hands.

'No natural light,' she said, and then she looked at her husband and smiled.

She opened the door for them.

Once they were inside, though, her mother said only good things. She walked around and touched the cupboards and opened them, she looked at the window fastenings and moved the table a little bit, looking underneath at its legs. She touched almost everything in the flat but she only said good things.

Her father hardly touched anything. He was too tall to get through the doors properly and he moved through the rooms, far away from the walls and the pieces of furniture that had come with the flat. He looked different, he put his hands in his pockets a lot and he often cleared his throat although he had nothing to say.

She watched them, feeling sad and wanting to say things. She seemed to always be on the edge of saying something. She tried to say things that would make them feel better but all she really wanted to say was I love you. She saw her father stand and look at the view and it was all she wanted to say.

Before they left, she saw her mother and father stand and look at the view together. They said a lot of little things to each other, about how it would look at night and how you needed to have a nice view. They didn't look at each other, just out through the window but she saw they were holding hands.

The next two weeks before she moved were strange. Her father started fixing little things of hers that had been broken for a while. Her mother cooked a lot of food for her and she remembered this long article she'd read about a family where the mother was dying of cancer and they knew she only had a while left. This article said that it had brought the family together and that they'd spent all the time they had with each other, it said that they'd touched each other more. She thought that this was true, in a little way, in her family right now. But she also thought that even though they felt closer, they really felt further apart. It hadn't said that in the article, she didn't remember it saying that. In the article it had said that they loved each other more. She knew it wasn't the same, she wasn't dying of cancer or anything like that, but she didn't think that they loved each other more because loving wouldn't feel like this. Loving would be laughing with nothing underneath. And now, though they hugged each other more, they didn't squeeze for a joke like they always had before. Against each other, their bodies were still.

She only talked to her boyfriend about it once. She told him about the article but she couldn't explain what it was she felt and, trying to make her feel better, he only said things that she already knew.

'They can come round all the time,' he said. 'I like them,' he said. 'It's not far away.'

And then he told her that he loved her. He looked into her face and he really told her, like he was trying to say something else. Like he was trying to say that because he loved her, that should make this other thing better. Like she should think about him loving her and that would make her feel good again.

It rained on the moving-out day, Easter Sunday, and the wind was very hard. They helped her carry her stuff down the road to the car, they stepped wide over the puddles. Her father walked beside her most of the time. His coat was blown against his legs and his face was bruised with the cold.

When it was finished, they ate Marmite sandwiches and they sat in the kitchen where it was warm and they could hear the central heating. By then it was getting dark outside. Sometimes, when the wind changed, they heard the rain against the kitchen window. They saw the grey shapes of the cherry tree's branches moving and they opened a bottle of wine. The kitchen was very tidy, they hadn't made a proper meal that day.

She wanted it to feel good, sitting with them for that last hour or so. Everything made her feel awkward, though. The photograph of her playing canasta that was stuck with Blu-tack on the wall. The way her mother poured her a glass of wine. And now she couldn't find much to say.

They talked about the little details. 'Did you get your shampoo?' her father said. 'There was a bottle of your shampoo by the bath. I don't know if you want to take that with you.' He stood with his back against the sink, held his wine glass loosely in both hands. Every time they said something like this, she was closer to having to go.

Across the table, her mother sat, smoking. She had her feet up on one of the chairs, her shoes were kicked to one side on the floor and she leaned back like she was tired. 'Bank Holiday tomorrow,' her mother said as she looked over at her father standing by the sink and smiled. Her empty hand lay flat on the table. 'We'll have a lie-in,' she said. She called him over with a tilt of her head, and when he moved towards her, she touched his side. She looked up at him like a child.

The kitchen light was yellow and soft on her skin, on the open bottle of wine. Above her father's head she saw a spot on the wall where the paint was starting to peel. It was white under this magnolia, he'd painted it a long time before. She remembered the sheets that had lain over everything and the paint on her father's hands. It might have been blue before that, she thought she could remember it being blue.

'Do you remember when we had that Easter egg hunt?' she said. 'And all the eggs had little notes around them and stuff. You did a note for each egg.' She wanted to show them she remembered it, that she remembered it as well as they did. 'The kitchen was blue then,' she said.

'They were clues,' her father said. '"If you want to find the treasure, look to the place where you're at leisure."'

'Under my pillow,' she said. She remembered that the chocolate had melted and the foil had stuck to it in pieces.

Her father was holding his glass in one hand now. 'Well, we always tried hard with the parties and stuff,' he said.

She nodded, saw her mother reach across and tap the cigarette. Now, she didn't want to leave. She thought about telling them that she was tired now and she might stay another night. But she was picking her boyfriend up at six thirty. He'd have his stuff all stacked up by the porch and he'd be waiting for her; he'd have that smile.

Across the table, her parents were close together. They looked at each other and then her father moved away. Her mother watched him, her feet still up on the chair, as he reached and opened a cupboard. She pushed a strand of hair away from her face. He said, 'We wanted to give you something.' He pulled it out of the cupboard. 'Don't get excited,' he said. 'We didn't buy it. It's not a new set of car keys or anything. Don't get excited.'

She started to say something about how they shouldn't have, about how they didn't have to get her anything at all, but she stopped halfway through talking. It didn't really sound right. It didn't sound like something she'd say to them.

Standing there, her father held it for a moment. In his hands, she couldn't see what it was. He had always had big hands. 'It's probably stupid,' her father said. 'You'll probably never use it for anything.'

'It isn't stupid,' her mother said. 'Don't say that. She won't think that.'

'It's from both of us,' he said. And then he put it down on the table. It was a little wooden box. It was old, she could see it was old. She didn't know what kind of wood it was made out of, she wasn't good with kinds of wood or anything like that. The box was plain, it looked small on the table and the yellow light from overhead put a soft touch across its lid.

'It's empty,' her father said. He leaned down and touched it again, he didn't push it towards her. 'Just in case you thought there was something in it.'

'We would've liked to have filled it with cash,' her mother said. And then she laughed, and then she shrugged. When no one said anything else, she said, 'Your father bought it when we moved in together, brought it back from a second-hand shop.'

She looked away from her mother's face, down at the box again. She reached out and felt that the wood was warm. Underneath the cupboards there were little striplights to light up the counters. They warmed up the bottoms of the cupboards. They had warmed the wooden box.

'Only cost twenty pence,' her father said.

Her mother said, 'I know people, like my sister, she's a good example, they think if you find something cheap then it can't be as good as if it cost hundreds of pounds. She's always been like that. I always thought that if you found something nice and it was a bargain then that made it even better.' Her mother watched as she opened the box and looked at its smooth empty wood.

'We wanted to put something in it,' her father said. 'I said some potpourri or something. I don't know. We left it empty.'

'We thought you'd probably find something. You know, something you wanted to put in there yourself. You can keep anything in it.'

She looked at the box. She opened and closed its lid. She looked up at her parents.

'He's a nice man,' her mother said. 'We're glad you've found a nice man.'

'I know.'

'He's a good guy,' her father said.

She looked at both of them. 'I love you,' she said.

They watched her touch the wooden box. She held it in both of her hands. She thought about her boyfriend, he'd be waiting with all his boxes. He'd be watching for her headlights outside.

They stayed together in the kitchen after their daughter left. They finished the bottle of wine. He watched her sit up and pull her shoes towards her with the point of one bare foot. The red varnish on her toenails was chipped. She always painted her toenails red.

'Well,' he said. He picked up the empty bottle and smiled. 'It's lasted well, that box,' he said. And then he said, 'Twenty pence.' She didn't look at him, she was putting on her shoes. 'It was that shop by the launderette,' he said. Still seated, bending down towards the ground, her hair fell across her face.

She stood up slowly and she saw him looking. The wine bottle was still in his hand.

'Here,' she said. She put her arms around his waist and felt the cold glass of the empty bottle settle against her back. He was warm. 'You're like a hot water bottle,' she said. She'd told him that a lot of times before, it was one of the things she said.

His voice was even. 'I love you.'

Looking over his shoulder, the kitchen counter was clean. She saw the biscuit tin and a shopping list for the supermarket tomorrow, on the back of an old envelope. And she held on to him very tightly then.

'I love you too,' she said.

In this new place, the overhead lights were bright, on the bare carpet, on the walls. The boxes were piled on top of each other and they had to squeeze between. She listened to him unpacking the bottle of wine and she moved between the little rooms. My bedroom, she thought, my bathroom. But it was the living room that sounded best, she thought. She said it, 'My living room.'

She walked through and saw him standing between the piles of battered cardboard boxes. He was holding two glasses in his hand.

'Our balcony,' she said. She pointed. The little balcony had two chairs on it, as though it was their view alone. The place smelled stale and airless; she still had her overcoat on.

'Have you seen the shelves?' he said. He showed her the dust marks on them, he showed her the clear even spaces where someone else's books had sat. On the walls there were empty picture hooks and they talked about what they were going to hang there and what had been there before. Everywhere she walked, he smiled at her.

'Do you think it was a couple that lived here?' she said. She thought that it must have been. He told her that he didn't care. He reached out and put a hand on her thigh, waiting, watching her face.

They drank a lot of wine that night; he filled the glasses before they were empty. They sat with their backs against the cardboard boxes or they lay together on the floor. They talked about how long they would live in this place. A year, or two years. The words sounded strange.

Later, when she was nearly drunk, she took out the little wooden box and she put it on the carpet between them. She talked about her parents and what they'd said. For a little while, she cried.

'It's a lovely box,' he said. 'They love you.'

And then he took the cork from next to the bottle of wine and he showed it to her, in his hand.

'You're only meant to do this with champagne corks,' he said.

He took out a handful of change from his trouser pocket and she watched him sort through it, smiling when he couldn't see. She loved him for the way he held his change. You make like a slit in the cork and you put the fifty-pence piece in. It's for good luck.' He looked up at her. 'It's tradition,' he said.

She watched him make it, moving his hands with his head bent over. Behind him, the wall was bare with the light. She would try to remember this.

'Why do you love me?' she said. She looked at the little wooden box. It was empty on the floor.

'I don't know.' His hands were still now. Outside, she could hear the sound of night traffic, tyres on the wet road. 'Because of the things you say to me.' He looked at her like he wanted it to be the right answer. 'Because of the way you make me feel.'

'Anyone who loved you would say those things.'

He looked away, at the cork he was holding between his fingers. After a moment, he passed it to her. He watched her take it and place it slowly in the wooden box. He watched it roll there in tiny, decreasing arcs.

In his lap, his hands were still. 'Because you chose me,' he said.

Author Biographies

Nicholas Blincoe is the pseudonym of a workers' collective active in publishing, journalism and related industries.

Story completed April 2000

Matthew Branton is the author of three novels: *The Love Parade* (1997), *The House of Whacks* (1999), *Coast* (2000). *The Hired Gun* will be published in spring 2001. He recently turned thirty and currently lives in Hawaii.

Story completed March 2000.

Candida Clark was born in 1970 and read Philosophy & English Literature at Cambridge. She has written two novels, *The Last Look* (1998) and *The Constant Eye* (2000), both published by Chatto & Windus. She is currently completing a third. She has recently been awarded a West Midlands Arts Fellowship at Warwick and currently lives in Oxford.

Story completed March 2000

Anna Davis grew up in Cardiff and now lives in London, where she works as a literary agent. She also teaches on the MA in Novel Writing at Manchester University. Her first two novels, *The Dinner* (1999) and *Melting* (2000), are published by Sceptre, and she is currently writing her third.

Story completed April 2000

Geoff Dyer is the author of three novels: *The Colour of Memory* (1989), *The Search* (1993), and *Paris Trance* (1998); a study of John Berger, *Ways of Telling* (1986); three genre-defying titles, *But Beautiful* (1991), *The Missing of the Somme* (1994) and *Out of Sheer Rage* (1997); and a collection of essays, *Anglo-English Attitudes* (1999). He is also co-editor, with Margaret Sartor, of *What Was True: The Photographs and Notebooks of William Gedney* (2000).

Story completed February 2000

Bo Fowler was born in 1971. He intends to write one hundred novels and then die. So far he has written only two: *Scepticism, Inc* (1998) and *The Astrological Diary of God* (1999). He is currently working on the remaining ninety-eight.

Story completed December 1999

Alex Garland was born in London in 1970. His first two books were *The Beach* (1997) and *The Tesseract* (1998).

Story completed January 2000

Daren King was born in 1972 in Harlow, Essex. He was educated at Bath Spa University College, Bath, where he graduated in Creative Studies. His first novel, *Boxy an Star* (1999), was shortlisted for the 1999 Guardian First Book Award.

Story completed February 2000

Simon Lewis was born in 1971. He has written a novel called *Go* (1999) and a guidebook to Beijing.

Story completed January 2000

Toby Litt was born in 1968 in Bedfordshire. He has had three books published: *Adventures in Capitalism* (1996), *Beatniks* (1997) and *Corpsing* (2000).

Story completed February 29th 2000

Rebbecca Ray lives in central London and is now on holiday. She is the author of *A Certain Age* (1998).

Story completed February 2000

Ben Richards was born in 1964 and lives in London. He has worked as a Housing Officer for Newham and Islington councils, and has lectured at the University of Birmingham. He is the author of four novels: *Throwing the House out of the Window* (1994), which won the Texaco Eastside Award for first-time novelists, *Don't Step on the Lines* (1997), *The Silver River* (1998) and *A Sweetheart Deal* (2000). He is currently working on his fifth novel. His work has also been featured in *The Face* and *The Agony and The Ecstasy – Short Stories and New Writing in Celebration of The World Cup* and various other anthologies.

Story completed March 2000

Scarlett Thomas is twenty-seven. She is the author of *Dead Clever* (1998) *In Your Face* (1999) and *Seaside* (1999), all featuring Lily Pascale. She is also the author of *Bright Young Things* (2000), a book about six people who wake up on an island and don't know why they are there. In her spare time, Scarlett designs web sites and plays a lot of video games.

Story completed February 2000

Matt Thorne was born in 1974. He is the author of *Tourist* (1998), *Eight Minutes Idle* (1999) and *Dreaming of Strangers* (2000).

Story completed November 1999

Tony White was born in 1964. He is the editor of the *Britpulp!* anthology (1999) and author of three novels: *Road Rage!* (1997), *Charlieunclenorfolktango* (1999) and *Satan! Satan! Satan!* (1999). He made London his home eleven years ago, has an eight-year-old son, and has worked in a variety of occupations – including a spell on the night shift in Royal Mail's North London sorting office. Currently Literary Editor for *The Idler* magazine, he lives and works in Whitechapel, East London.

Story completed February 2000

All Fourth Estate books are available from
your local bookshop.

Or visit the Fourth Estate website at:

www.4thestate.co.uk